Dear Reader,

Once upon a time, I was asked to contribute a book to a themed fairy-tale month. I jumped at the chance, but...which one? I scoured the internet and found hundreds of fascinating tales from across the world (not all compatible with romance!) before eventually settling on "Goldilocks and the Three Bears."

How about a fair-haired heroine who snacks on oat bars and for whom everything has to be just right? I mused. Named Orla ("golden princess"), perhaps. What if she's woken up in a bed she shouldn't be in by a darkly brooding bear of a hero who is still tormented by the loss of his wife and son, and isn't at all pleased to find her there? Shenanigans would ensue, I was sure. Heads would butt (quite literally!). And eventually, of course, love would prevail.

The result is *Undone by Her Ultra-Rich Boss*, and I hope you enjoy reading Duarte and Orla's story as much as I loved writing it.

*Lucy* xx

**Lucy King** spent her adolescence lost in the glamorous and exciting world of Harlequin when she really ought to have been paying attention to her teachers. But as she couldn't live in a dreamworld forever, she eventually acquired a degree in languages and an eclectic collection of jobs. After a decade in southwest Spain, Lucy now lives with her young family in Wiltshire, England. When not writing or trying to think up new and innovative things to do with mince, she spends her time reading, failing to finish cryptic crosswords and dreaming of the golden beaches of Andalucia.

### Books by Lucy King

### Harlequin Presents

#### *Passion in Paradise*

*A Scandal Made in London*

#### *Lost Sons of Argentina*

*The Secrets She Must Tell*
*Invitation from the Venetian Billionaire*
*The Billionaire without Rules*

Visit the Author Profile page
at Harlequin.com for more titles.

# Lucy King

## UNDONE BY HER ULTRA-RICH BOSS

# PRESENTS

Recycling programs
for this product may
not exist in your area.

ISBN-13: 978-1-335-73852-3

Undone by Her Ultra-Rich Boss

Copyright © 2022 by Lucy King

For questions and comments about the quality of this book,
please contact us at CustomerService@Harlequin.com.

Harlequin Enterprises ULC
22 Adelaide St. West, 41st Floor
Toronto, Ontario M5H 4E3, Canada
www.Harlequin.com

**Printed in U.S.A.**

# UNDONE BY HER ULTRA-RICH BOSS

For Charlotte, editor extraordinaire

# CHAPTER ONE

*'QUEM ÉS TU e que raios fazes na minha cama?'*

In response to the deep, masculine, insanely sexy voice that penetrated the fog of sleep enveloping her, Orla Garrett let out an involuntary but happy little sigh and burrowed deeper into the cocoon of beautifully crisp, cool sheets she'd created for herself.

Duarte de Castro e Bragança usually paid her dreams a visit the night following the day they'd spoken on the phone. Every time his name popped up on the screen her stomach fluttered madly. The ensuing conversation, during which his velvety yet gravelly tones sent shivers racing up and down her spine, unfailingly left every nerve-ending she possessed buzzing.

They'd never met in person and their calls weren't particularly noteworthy—she ran an ultra-exclusive invitation-only concierge business of which he was a member, so they generally involved his telling her what he wanted and her assuring him it would be done—but that didn't seem to matter. Her subconscious inevitably set his voice to the photos that frequently appeared in the press and which she, along with probably every other hot-blooded person on the planet, couldn't help but notice, and went into overdrive.

It was unusual to be dreaming of him now when she hadn't spoken to him in over a month. Even stranger that he was speaking in his native Portuguese when he only ever addressed her in the faintly accented yet flawless English he'd acquired thanks to a British public school education, followed by Oxford.

But she knew from experience that there was little she could do to prevent it, and really, why would she want to even try? The moves he made on her... The way she woke up hot and breathless and trembling from head to toe... It was as close as she got to the real thing these days, not that the real thing had ever been any good in her albeit limited experience, which was why she gave it such a wide berth.

Besides, there was no harm in a dream. It wasn't as if she harboured the secret hope that the things he did to her would ever become reality. The very idea of it was preposterous.

Firstly, quite apart from the fact that she steered well clear of things she wasn't any good at, getting involved that way with a client—any client—would be highly unprofessional.

Secondly, there was no way a staggeringly handsome, fast-living aristocratic billionaire winemaker would ever notice her in the unlikely event they did get round to meeting.

And finally, the entire world knew how devoted reformed playboy Duarte had been to his beautiful wife and how devastated he'd been when she'd died of an overdose six weeks after giving birth to their stillborn son, even if he was now reported to be handling the double tragedy with unbelievable stoicism.

No, her dreams were private, safe and, even better, unlike reality, completely devoid of the hyper-critical voice that lived in her head, constantly reminding her of how much she had to do and how, if she wanted to feel good about herself, she must not fail at any of it. In the dreams that featured Duarte, perfection wasn't something to strive for; it was a given.

'Hello,' she mumbled into a gorgeous pillow that was neither too hard nor too soft but just right.

'I said, who are you and what the hell are you doing in my bed?'

This time he did speak in English, his spine-tingling voice a fraction closer now, and, as a trace of something deliciously spicy wafted up her nose and into her head, warmth stole through her and curled her toes.

'Waiting for you,' she murmured while wondering with a flicker of excitement what he might do next.

Thanks to a last-minute let-down, she'd been working flat out for the past week, preparing his estate for the annual meeting of the world's top five family-owned wine-producing businesses. Her exhaustion ran deep. Her muscles ached. A massage, even an imaginary one, would be heavenly.

'Get up. Now.'

Well, that wasn't very nice, was it? Unlike those of Dream Duarte, who generally smouldered and purred at her before drawing her into a scorchingly hot clinch, these words were brusque. This Duarte sounded annoyed. Impatient. Where was the smile? Why was the hand on her shoulder shaking her hard instead of kneading and caressing? And, come to think of it, why could she smell him so vividly? His scent had never been part of her dreams before...

Realisation started off as a trickle, which swiftly became a torrent, and then turned into a tsunami, crashing through her like a wrecking ball and smashing the remnants of sleep to smithereens.

With her heart slamming against her ribs, Orla sat bolt upright and cracked her head against something hard. Pain lanced through her skull and she let out a howl of agony that was matched in volume by a thundering volley of angry Portuguese which accompanied a sudden lurch of the mattress.

Ow, ow, *ow*.

God, that hurt.

Jerking back, she clutched her forehead, rubbing away the stars while frantically blinking back the sting of tears, until the pounding in her head finally ebbed to a dull throb and the urge to bawl receded.

If only the same could be said for the shock and mortification pulsating through her. If only she could fling herself back under the covers and pretend this wasn't happening with equal success. But unfortunately she couldn't and it was, so gingerly, with every cell of her being cringing in embarrassment and horror, she opened her eyes.

At the sight of the man sitting hunched on the bed, shaking his head and running his hands through his dark, unruly hair, her breath caught. She went hot, then cold, then hot again. Her stomach flipped and her pulse began to race even faster.

Yes, Duarte was actually here, very much *not* a figment of her imagination, and oh, dear lord, this was *awful*. He'd caught her asleep on the job. She'd all but invited him to join her in bed. And then she'd headbutted him—her most important, wealthiest client—and that was saying something when to even be considered deserving of an invitation their members had to have a minimum net worth of half a billion dollars.

At least she'd kept her clothes on when, energy finally depleted, she'd crashed out, which was a mercy, even if they were on the skimpy side, since it was hot in the Douro Valley in June. But how on *earth* was she going to redeem herself?

That he hadn't been expected back for another three weeks was no excuse. Her company promised perfection on every level. Their clients demanded—and paid outrageously for—the very best. This was the absolute worst, most mortifying situation she could have ever envisaged.

'I'm so sorry,' she breathed shakily, deciding that grovelling would be a good place to start as she pulled up the spaghetti strap of her T-shirt, which had slipped off her shoulder and down her arm.

Duarte snapped his head round, his dark gaze colliding with hers, and the breath was whipped from her lungs all over again. The pictures she'd seen of him in the press didn't do him justice. Not even slightly. They didn't capture the size or presence of the man, let alone his vital masculinity, which hit her like a blow to the chest and instantly fired parts of her body she hadn't even known existed. They didn't accurately reflect the breadth of his shoulders or the power of his jean-clad thighs that, she noticed as her palms began to sweat, were within touching distance. Nor did she recall ever seeing in any photo quite such cold fury blazing in the obsidian depths of his eyes or a jaw so tight it looked as if it were about to shatter.

'Can I get you some ice for your head?' she managed, inwardly wincing at the memory of how hard she'd crashed against him before remembering the emergency first-aid kit that she kept in her bag just in case. 'Painkillers, perhaps?'

'No,' he growled, his expression as black as night, tension evident in every line of his body. 'You can answer my question.'

Right. Yes. She should do that. Because now was not the time to be getting caught up in his darkly compelling looks that were having such a strangely intense effect on her. Now was the time for damage control.

'My name is Orla Garrett,' she said, praying that despite his evident anger Duarte was nevertheless reasonable enough to see the amusing side of the situation once she explained. With the exception of this lapse in professionalism, the service her company provided him with was excellent and that had to count for something. 'I'm co-owner and joint CEO of Hamilton Garrett. We've spoken on the phone.'

His brows snapped together and she could practically see his reportedly razor-sharp brain spinning as he raked his gaze over her in a way that made her flood with heat.

Should she hold out her hand for him to shake? she wondered, a bit baffled by the electricity that was suddenly sizzling through her. Somehow, with her still beneath the sheets and him still sitting on top of them not even a foot away, it didn't seem appropriate.

Far more urgent was the desire to surge forwards and settle herself on his lap. Then she could sift her fingers through his hair and check his head for bumps. She could run her hands over his face and examine first his impressive bone structure and then the faint stubble adorning his jaw. At that point he could wrap his arms round her and flip her over, set his mouth to her neck and—

Agh.

What was happening? What was she thinking? Was she *nuts*?

Appalled by the wayward direction in which her thoughts were hurtling but deciding to blame it on possible concussion, Orla swallowed hard and pulled herself together. She had to ignore the scorching fire sweeping along her veins and the all too vivid images cascading into her head, the reasons for which she could barely comprehend. There'd be time for analysis later. Right now, she needed to put some space between her and her client, so she scrambled off the bed on the other side and onto her feet.

'As per your instructions,' she said, fighting for dignity, for control, and smoothing shorts that suddenly felt far too tight and uncomfortably itchy, 'I've been preparing the guest accommodation for your conference. So far, all the bedrooms are ready except this one.'

Which was the one that looked to require the least work. The other five had been complete tips. Bed and bath linen had been left awry and crusty wine glasses had been abandoned on surfaces thick with dust. Downstairs had fared no better. Coffee cups overspilling with mould had littered the drawing room and empty wine bottles had filled a crate in the kitchen.

Trying not to gag at the smell, Orla had wondered what on earth had been going on here before reminding herself sternly that it was none of her business. Her job was to see that her clients' wishes were fulfilled and that was it.

'I've agreed the menus for the weekend with Mariana Valdez,' she said, hauling her thoughts back in line and focusing on the tiny stab of triumph she felt at having acquired the only chef in the world to currently hold ten Michelin stars, who was virtually impossible to hire for a private function, 'and all dietary requirements will be catered for. I've instructed Nuno Esteves,' the Quinta's chief vintner, 'to make available the wines you stipulated for dinner on the Friday and Saturday nights. The river cruise has been scheduled for the Sunday afternoon and the crew is prepping the boat as we speak. Everything is on track.'

Duarte shifted round to glower at her, clearly—and unfairly—unimpressed by what she'd accomplished under very trying circumstances. 'And all the while you've been sleeping in my bed.'

'No,' she said with a quick, embarrassed glance at the rumpled sheets, which didn't help her composure at all. 'I haven't. I booked into the hotel in the village, and I've been staying there. The nap was a one-off, I swear. Not that that makes it any better. It's unforgivable, I know.'

Not to mention inexcusable, even though excuses abounded. Duarte wouldn't be remotely interested in the fact that she'd been let down at the last minute by the team she'd put in place to carry out his requests and had had no option but to see to the situation herself, however inconvenient and however long the hours. It wasn't his problem that she'd somehow found herself in possession of the wrong set of keys and had had to break a window to get in so she could unlock the back door from the inside and proceed from there. Like all their clients, he paid a six-figure annual fee to have his every instruction carried out, without question, without issue, free from hassle and the tedious minutiae of implementation.

'I can assure you that it will never happen again,' she finished, mentally crossing her fingers and willing him to overlook the blip. 'You have my word.'

He let out a harsh laugh, as if unable to believe her word counted for anything. Then he gave his head a slow shake, at which her pulse thudded and panic swelled, because as the dragging seconds ticked silently by she got the sickening feeling that he wasn't going to forgive. He wasn't going to forget. The tension in his jaw wasn't easing and his mouth wasn't curving into a smile as she'd hoped. The anger in his dark, magnetic gaze might be fading but the emptiness that remained was possibly even worse. His expression was worryingly unfathomable and his voice, when he spoke, was icy cold.

'You're right,' he said with a steely grimness that made her throat tighten and her heart plunge. 'It *won't* happen again. Because you're fired.'

Duarte barely registered the soft gasp of the woman standing beside the bed, staring down at him with the mesmerising eyes the colour of fifty-year-old tawny port that had sent a jolt rocketing through him when they'd first made contact with his. He hardly noticed the way she tensed and jerked back, her expression revealing shock and dawning dismay.

He couldn't think straight. His head throbbed from the earlier collision. His chest was tight and his muscles were tense to the point of snapping. It was taking every drop of his control to repel the harrowing memories that had been triggered by setting foot in this house for the first time in nearly three years. To contain the savage emotions that were battering him on all sides.

Frustration and surprise that his instructions had not been carried out correctly warred with fury that his fiercely protected privacy had been invaded. Shock on finding a beautiful, golden-haired woman fast asleep in his bed clashed with horror at the desire that had slammed into him out of nowhere at the sight of her. The grief and guilt that he'd buried deep had surged up and smashed through his defences and were now blindsiding him with their raw, unleashed intensity.

None of it was welcome. Not the swirling emotions, not the clamouring memories of his difficult, deceitful wife and tiny, innocent son who had never got to draw a breath, and certainly not the unexpectedly gorgeous Orla Garrett here, in his space, wrecking the status quo and demolishing the equilibrium he strove so hard to maintain.

'I'm sorry?' she said, sounding dazed and breathless in a way that to his frustration made him suddenly acutely aware of the bed, and had him leaping to his feet.

'You heard,' he snapped, striding to the window and shoving his hands into the pockets of his jeans before whipping round. 'You're fired.'

Her astonishing eyes widened. 'Because I took a nap?'

The reasons were many, complicated and tumultuous, and very much not for sharing. 'Because you're clearly incompetent.'

Her chin came up and her jaw tightened. 'I am many things, I will admit, but incompetent is not one of them.'

'Then what would you call this?' he said, yanking a hand out of his pocket and waving it to encompass the bed, the room, the house.

She flushed. 'A lapse.'

'It's more than that.'

'The circumstances are extenuating.'

'And irrelevant.'

She stared at him for a moment, frowning, as if debating with herself, then she took a deep breath and gave a brief nod.

'You're right,' she said with enviable self-possession. 'I can't apologise enough for all of this. For hitting you in the head and, before that, implying that I was waiting for you. Obviously, I wasn't. I was asleep. Dreaming. About someone else entirely.'

Who? was the question that instantly flew into his thoughts like the sharpest of arrows. A husband?

A lover? And what the hell was that thing suddenly stabbing him in the chest? Surely it couldn't be *disappointment*? That would be ridiculous.

Despite having spoken to Orla frequently over the last few years, which had presumably given her an insight into certain aspects of his life, he knew next to nothing about her. But that was fine. He didn't need to. Their relationship, if one could even call it that, was strictly business.

Whether or not she was single was of no interest to him. So what if her voice at the other end of the line had recently begun to stir something inside him he'd thought long dead? Given that he'd sworn off women for the foreseeable future, the wounds caused by his short but ill-fated marriage still savagely raw, it was intrusive and annoying and not to be encouraged.

'You've been working on the wrong place,' he said, angered by the unacceptable direction of his thoughts when he worked so hard to keep them under control.

'What do you mean?'

'I instructed you to fix up the accommodation at the winery. This is not the winery.'

Her brows snapped together. 'I don't understand.'

'This is Casa do São Romão, not Quinta do São Romão. So you've broken into what was once, briefly, my home. You've been poking your nose into places where you do not belong and sleeping in my bed. And in the meantime, the task I *did* assign you remains unfulfilled.'

She stared at him, confusion written all over her lovely face. 'What?'

'You've made a mistake, Ms Garrett,' he said grimly, although actually, to call Orla's actions 'a mistake' was an understatement. She'd invaded his space. Whether she knew it or not, she'd seen things he'd never intended anyone to see. Not even *he* had ever again wanted to have to confront the evidence of his torment, his grief and his guilt, which he'd indulged at length before locking away for ever. If this house had been left to rack and ruin, taking with it the memories contained within and turning them to dust, that would have been fine with him.

But at least the contract between him and Orla's company had come with an NDA. At least the truth about his supposedly perfect marriage would never emerge. The thought of it brought him out in a cold sweat. He judged himself plenty. He didn't need judgement from anywhere else.

'I can't have,' said Orla, visibly blanching, evidently stunned.

'Are you suggesting it's *I* who's made the mistake?'

'What? N-no. Of course not,' she stammered, the blush hitting her cheeks turning them from deathly pale to a pretty pink. 'There must have been a communication error. I'm so sorry. I'll make this right.'

There was nothing she could do to make anything

right. What was done could not be undone. He should know. His son couldn't be reborn with a heartbeat instead of without one. He couldn't rewind time so that he could both erase the argument that had caused that and subsequently see what was happening with Calysta in time to stop her taking her own life. No one could. What he *could* do was get rid of Orla before he lost his grip on his fast-unravelling control.

'You have five minutes to get your things,' he said, his voice low and tight with the effort of holding himself together when inside he was being torn apart, 'and then I want you gone.'

# CHAPTER TWO

Rooted to the spot, Orla watched Duarte turn on his heel and stride off, her heart hammering and a cold sweat breaking out all over her skin. The floor beneath her feet seemed to be rocking and the room was spinning.

Oh, God, he was furious. He clearly didn't tolerate mistakes and she couldn't blame him, because neither did she. In fact, she hadn't made a single one since her engagement, which had come to an end four years ago. And even *before* that she'd done her level best to avoid them. Mistakes equalled failure and failure was not an option in her world.

As an overlooked, average middle child squashed between an older sister who sang like an angel and a brilliant athlete of a younger brother, she'd fought hard for her space in the family. She'd worked like a demon to get the best grades at school and siphon off some of the parental attention her more talented, more successful siblings attracted so easily. And it had worked. So well, in fact, that striving for excellence, for perfection, had become embedded in her DNA. Her sense of self-worth depended on it, she knew, and she couldn't imagine ever approaching a task with the expectation of anything less.

But she hadn't allowed her childhood insecurities to surge up and swamp her for years, and she certainly wasn't about to start now. Her blood chilled at the very idea of it. So it didn't matter at this precise moment how the mix-up here had happened when her company went to great lengths to ensure a project ran as smoothly as possible. An analysis of what had gone wrong would have to wait.

Nor was her opinion of Duarte's reaction to the situation of any relevance. She might think that his response was totally over-the-top when firstly, she'd never let him down before, secondly, there was still time to fix things, and finally, he had the unexpected bonus of a freshly gleaming home, but he was the client. He was clearly furious that she'd screwed up—although he couldn't possibly be as angry with her as she was with herself—and it was her job to reverse that. To get herself unfired. And not just because she had two decades' worth of hang-ups to battle. After years of grafting to prove her talent, her worth and her indispensability, of single-mindedly focusing on reaching the top, she'd finally been allowed to buy into the business. She had no intention of giving Sam, co-owner and joint CEO of Hamilton Garrett, any reason to regret that decision. Duarte earned them millions in fees and commissions—almost as much as all their other clients put together—and she would *not* be the one to lose him.

It wouldn't be easy but nor was it impossible. The coldness of his tone—worse than if he'd shouted at her, in fact—wasn't encouraging, but all she'd have to do, surely, was handle him the way she handled anyone who was reluctant to give her what she wanted. People always saw things her way in the end, and he'd be no different.

Taking a deep breath to calm the panic and channelling cool determination instead, Orla grabbed her trainers and strode out of the bedroom. She raced around the balcony that looked over the ground floor on all four sides of the house, until she came to the top of the wide, sweeping stone staircase.

'Wait,' she called, spying Duarte heading along a corridor, and hurrying down the steps. But he didn't stop, he didn't even show any sign he'd heard her, so she tried again. Louder. 'Conde de Castro. Duarte. Please. Stop. I can explain.'

He threw up a dismissive hand. 'No.'

'I'll do anything. Just name it.'

'It's too late.'

It couldn't be. That wasn't an option. 'How can I make this right?'

'You can't.'

She could. She *would*. She just had to figure out what he wanted. A discount, perhaps. Didn't everyone love a bargain, even wildly successful billionaires? 'I'll waive your fees for the next three years. Five. No, *ten*.'

'Your fees are a rounding error to me,' he said bluntly, continuing to power ahead with long, loose strides while she, still barefoot, remained hot on his heels. 'And if you think I'm continuing with my membership of your organisation, you are, once again, very much mistaken.'

Right. Not that, then. 'I'll make a donation to a charity of your choice.'

'You couldn't possibly match the sums I already donate.'

That was undoubtedly true.

*Damn*.

'I'll have someone else handle your account,' she offered, ignoring the odd sense of resistance that barrelled through her at the thought of it because desperate times called for desperate measures.

'No.'

Well, good. But on the other hand, not good. In the face of such intractability, she had little to work with here and she could feel the panic begin to return, but she banked it down because she wasn't giving up.

'Could you stop for a moment so we can talk about this?' she said, fighting to keep the desperation from her voice and thinking that while his back view— broad shoulders, trim waist—was a fine sight, it would be a whole lot easier to persuade him to see things her way if they were face to face.

'There's nothing to discuss.'

'Have we ever let you down before?'

'You've let me down now.'

'Your conference isn't for another three weeks. There's more than enough time to prepare.' Just about.

'That's not the point.'

Then what *was* the point? None of this made any sense. Yes, she'd made a mistake, and she winced just to think of it, but objectively speaking, it was hardly the end of the world. So what was going on? At no point during the course of their relationship had Duarte come across as in any way eccentric. His requests were by no means as outrageous as some. Quite the opposite in fact. She'd always considered him entirely reasonable.

So could it be that he was just stubborn? Well, so was she. She stood to lose not just his business and her partner's respect and confidence in her but also quite possibly her emotional equilibrium, which relied on her continually succeeding at everything she did, and that wasn't happening.

'There must be *something* I can do to persuade you to change your mind,' she said, breathless with the effort of keeping up with him and adrenalin-fuelled alarm. 'Something you want.'

'There isn't.'

There was. Everyone had at least one weakness, and Duarte wasn't *that* godlike.

*Think*, she told herself as she continued to hurry after him. She had to think. What did he want that he didn't already have that only she could get him? What would he find irresistible? Impossible to refuse?

Desperately, Orla racked her brains for what she knew about him. She frantically sifted through a mental catalogue of interviews and articles, revisiting the phone conversations they'd had, grasping for titbits of information, for something, for *anything*…

Until—

Aha!

She had it. Thank *God*. The perfect challenge. It wouldn't be easy. In fact, it would most likely be immensely difficult, otherwise he'd already have achieved it. But making the impossible possible was her job. She had her methods. She had her sources. She frequently had to get creative and think flexibly. She'd find a way. She always did.

'How about a bottle of Chateau Lafite 1869?'

If Duarte had a fully functioning brain or any sense of self-preservation, he'd be sticking with his plan to shut this place back up and get the hell out of here so he could regroup and reset the status quo that had been shattered when he'd been informed that there was activity up at the house.

He'd only been back on the estate half an hour before the news had reached him. He hadn't waited to hear the details. His intention to spend the evening among the vines, which calmed his thoughts and grounded him in a way that nothing else could these days, had evaporated. A dark, swirling mist had descended, wiping his head of reason and accelerating his pulse, and he'd driven straight here, leaving in his wake a cloud of clay-filled dust.

He'd assumed whoever it was had broken in. He'd been fuelled by fury and braced for a fight. Then he'd found her, a golden-haired stranger in his bed, and the mist had thickened. Women had been known to go to great lengths to attract his attention. His wife, who'd gone to the greatest lengths of all by deliberately falling pregnant and effectively trapping him into marriage, had been one of them. So what did this one want?

The discovery of Orla's identity had cleared some of the mist, but it had made no difference whatsoever to his intention to eject her from his existence. He never deviated from a plan once made, whether it be a seduction, a marriage proposal or perpetuating a lie in order to assuage his guilt. Yet now, unhinged and battered, and with the name of the wine he'd been after for years and the whisper of promise hovering in the ether, he came to an abrupt halt and whipped round.

'What are you talking about?'

For a moment Orla just stared at him as if she hadn't a clue either, breathless and flushed, but a second later she folded her arms and squared her shoulders.

'You think I'm incompetent,' she said, her chin up and her eyes lit with a fire that turned them to a daz-

zling burnished gold and momentarily robbed him
of his wits. 'Let me prove to you I'm not. I read in
an article a while back that the only material thing
you want but don't have is an 1869 bottle of Chateau Lafite. I will get it for you. Give me twenty-
four hours.'

Incredulity obliterated the dazzle and the return
of his reason slammed him back to earth. Seriously?
She thought it was that easy? She had *no* idea. He'd
been trying to get his hands on this wine, without
success, for years. He'd tried everything. Persuasion,
negotiation…he'd even toyed with the idea of brib-
ery. What could she achieve in twenty-four hours?
A couple of phone calls. That would be it.

'It's an exceptionally rare vintage,' he said scath-
ingly, unable to keep the disbelief from his voice.

'I wouldn't expect it to be anything less.'

'Only three bottles exist.'

She stared at him for the longest of seconds,
blanching faintly. 'Three?'

'Three,' he confirmed with a nod. 'And none of
the owners is interested in selling.'

'Well,' she said, straightening her spine in an obvious attempt to recover. 'Not to you, maybe.'

But they would to her? What planet was she on?
Delusion? 'You must be mad.'

'I've never felt saner.'

No. The colour had returned to her cheeks and
her gaze now was filled with cool determination.
She looked very sure of herself. Whereas he'd never

felt *less* on solid ground. Spinning round like that
had put him too close to her. Every cell of his body
quivered with awareness. He could make out a ring
of brown at the outer edges of her golden irises. Her
scent—something light and floral, gardenia, perhaps, subtly layered with notes of rose and possibly sea salt—was intoxicating. The blood pumping
through his veins was thick and sluggish. The need
to touch her burned so strongly inside him that he
had to shove his hands through his hair and take a
quick step back before his already weakened control
snapped and he acted on it.

'What makes you so sure you'll succeed where I
didn't?' he said, crushing the inappropriate and unwelcome lunacy, and focusing.

'Experience,' she said. 'Tenacity. Plus, I never
fail.'

Orla's tone was light but he detected a note of steel
in her voice, which suggested a story that would have
piqued his curiosity had he been remotely interested
in finding out what it might be. But he wasn't. All
he wanted was to forget that this afternoon had ever
happened and get back to burying the guilt and the
regret beneath a Mount Everest of a workload and
getting through the days.

And in any case, she wouldn't be around long
enough to ask even if he *was*. While he had to admire
her confidence—however misguided—she would
fail at this challenge and when the twenty-four hours
were up she would leave. Which would mean hav-

ing to find someone else to prepare the winery for the conference, but rare was the problem in business that couldn't be solved with money.

If it came to it, he would pay whatever it took. The conference was too important to screw up. Each year, in the belief that a rising tide lifted all boats, representatives from the world's top five family-owned wine businesses got together to analyse global trends, to solve any viticulture issues that might have arisen and generally to discuss all things oenological. This year it was his turn to host, the first since he'd taken his place as CEO three and a half years ago when the news that he was going to be a father had ignited an unexpected sense of responsibility inside him, which his own father had taken advantage of to retire.

There were those who couldn't see beyond the tabloid headlines and expected him to run the company into the ground by selling off all the assets and blowing the lot on having a good time, despite the twenty per cent increase in profit that had been generated since he'd been in charge. He didn't give a toss about them. He did, however, care about the business that had been going for nearly three hundred years. Its continued success depended on what people thought of his wines, and he was part of that package. He wasn't about to give anyone a reason to trash either his reputation or that of his company.

'So do we have a deal?' she said, jolting him out of his murky thoughts and recapturing his attention. 'Do you agree that if I succeed in acquiring this bottle of wine for you by this time tomorrow, you will recognise how good I am at my job and un-fire me?'

No, was the answer to that particular question. Orla had had her chance and she'd blown it. Duarte had a plan and he intended to stick to it. No allowances. No compromises. He'd been there, done that during his relationship with Calysta, regularly excusing her sometimes outrageous behaviour and ultimately sacrificing his freedom for what he'd believed to be the right thing, and he'd sworn he would never put himself in that position again.

Yet what if she did somehow succeed? he couldn't help wondering somewhere in the depths of his brain where recklessness still lurked. He'd be in possession of a bottle of the wine he'd been after for years. The headache of having to find someone else to finish the job she'd started would vanish. And then there was the sizzling attraction that was heating his blood and firing parts of his body he'd thought long numb and clamoured to be addressed.

Despite the reputation he'd earned in his twenties—which had been wholly deserved, he wasn't ashamed to admit—Duarte had no interest in romance these days. Love was a minefield into which he had no intention of venturing. It was messy and chaotic and could cause untold pain and resentment. In the wrong hands, it could be dangerous and damaging. Unrequited, it could be desperate and destructive.

Not that he'd ever experienced it himself. He'd

married Calysta because she was pregnant. A strange sense of duty he'd been totally unaware of previously had compelled him to stand by her and give their child his name. He'd never forget the moment he learned her pregnancy wasn't accidental, as he'd been led to believe. They'd been arguing about their lifestyle. He'd been determined to knuckle down and live up to his new responsibilities, she'd wanted to continue raising hell. In the heat of the moment, she'd yelled that she wished she'd stayed on the pill, and Duarte's world had stopped. He'd demanded an explanation, which she'd given, and at that moment any respect he'd had for her as the mother of his child had been blown to smithereens. He'd been taken for a fool, betrayed, his ability to trust pulverised, and the scars ran deep.

But it had been over three years since he'd slept with anyone, which was a long time for a man whose bedroom had once had a metaphorical revolving door. So perhaps that was why he was so aware of the flush on Orla's cheeks, the fire in her eyes and the way her chest still heaved with the effort of having raced to catch up with him. Maybe that was why he could so easily envisage her in his bed again, only this time with her wavy golden hair spread across his pillow as she gazed up at him, desire shining in her stunning topaz eyes and an encouragingly sultry smile curving her lovely mouth, focusing wholly on him instead of dreaming about someone else. If she was around, he'd have the opportunity to investigate this further and perhaps put an end to the sexual drought he'd been experiencing.

So, all things considered, he thought as the strands of these arguments wove together to form a conclusion, the pros of agreeing to her audacious proposal outweighed the cons. Changing the plan would be strategic, not weak. There'd be no need for compromises or allowances. The power, the control, would all be his.

'We have a deal.'

# CHAPTER THREE

ORLA HAD LEFT Duarte's house with a longer to-do list than she'd had going in, but as she'd carted her things to the hire car she'd parked round the back first thing she'd refused to entertain the possibility of not getting through it.

She had to pour all her energy into delivering on her promise, she'd told herself resolutely, firing up the engine and driving away. She had to temporarily forget the fact that her job and all that was attached to it hung in the balance. She couldn't afford to panic. She needed all her wits about her if she was going to achieve what would no doubt turn out to be her toughest challenge to date.

The minute she'd arrived back at her hotel, after paying the site of the old winery a visit to scope out the venue she should have been focusing on, she'd called the office back in London. On learning, to her distress, that the mistake had been entirely hers, she'd doubled down on her efforts to fix it.

She didn't know how or why she'd misread the

email that contained the details of Duarte's instructions but she hadn't wasted time dwelling on it. Instead, she'd been spurred into action. Since the Quinta was three times the size of the Casa and time was marching on, she'd sourced and hired a team from a local company to prepare it. A company new to her and an untested team, she'd recognised, but she had no doubt that she would be there to supervise.

Once that had been sorted, she'd set about tracking down the wine, which had been as challenging as she'd assumed. Although she reckoned she'd done a good job of concealing the sheer panic that had surged through her at Duarte's revelation that only three bottles of the wine he wanted existed, her confidence had been knocked for six. But she'd kept her cool, and on learning subsequently that all three bottles had been sold individually at auction fifteen years ago, she'd rallied. She knew the auctioneers well, and a ten-minute phone call had eventually furnished her with details of the sales.

The owners of the bottles she'd traced to Zurich and New York hadn't budged for anything. As for the bottle located in France, well, that had been a tough negotiation too, but ultimately a successful one— thank *God*—and as a result she was back at the top of her game, which was where she intended to stay.

There was no possible way that this evening Duarte would have the same impact on her as he had yesterday, she assured herself as she marched through the former manufacturing section of the winery, passing between rows of oak barrels that reached the roof and breathing in the rich scent of port that permeated the musty air. Those circumstances had been extraordinary, brought on by shock and, when he'd whipped round to face her in the corridor, so fast and unexpectedly she'd nearly crashed into him for the second time, the kind of proximity that punched her hard in the gut and flooded her with heat.

He'd looked at her for the longest of moments, she recalled, feeling a flush wash over her before she could stop it. That dark, hostile gaze of his had fixed to hers as if trying to see into her soul, and weirdly, time had seemed to stop. Her surroundings had receded and her focus had narrowed until all she could see was him. Her breasts had tightened and her mouth had gone dry. She'd felt very peculiar. Sort of on fire, yet shivery at the same time, and it had taken every ounce of strength to haul herself under control.

These circumstances, however, were anything but extraordinary. Given that they'd arranged this meeting an hour ago, there'd be no surprises. No head butts or strange spells of dizziness. No stopping of time, no galloping pulse and certainly no tingling of body parts. Her job was safe. She'd achieved the impossible and proved her value to him—and more importantly, to herself—and that was all that mattered.

Coming to a stop at the threshold of the room in which he'd told her to meet him, Orla pulled her shoulders back and took a deep breath. The anticipation and adrenalin crashing through her were entirely expected. The success of a project was always a rush, and with the added pressure of this one, and the sky-scraping stakes, the high was even higher.

On a slow, steadying exhale, she knocked on the door and at the curt *'Entra'* opened it. The room appeared to be half-office, half-sitting room. She briefly noticed a sofa, a coffee table, a sideboard and a pair of filing cabinets, but then her gaze landed on Duarte and yet again everything except him faded away.

He was sitting behind a desk, all large and shadowy, with the setting sun streaming in through the open window behind him and bathing the room in warm, golden light. If she'd been able to tear her eyes away from him she might have admired the twinkling river that wound through the landscape and the gently undulating hills beyond, their terraces covered with vines that were dense with verdant foliage stretching to the horizon. She might have found serenity in the big, airy room with its cool flagstone floor and rough, whitewashed walls.

But to her bewilderment and distress she couldn't look away. She couldn't focus on anything but him. He was just so magnetic, so compelling, and now she was feeling anything but triumphant, anything but serene. Her skin was prickling and oxygen seemed to be scarce. The linen shift dress she was wearing was by no means tight—in fact, she'd deliberately chosen it because of its loose-fitting nature—yet when the fabric brushed against her body, shivers ran down her spine. She felt strangely on edge, alert and primed, as if waiting for something to happen, although she couldn't for the life of her work out what.

'Do you have it?'

The deep timbre of his voice scraped over her nerve endings, weakening her knees dangerously, and for a moment she wondered, did she have what? Her marbles? Her self-possession? Apparently not. Because despite her hopes and expectations to the contrary, his effect on her was still so intense she could barely recall her own name. The X-rated dreams that had invaded what little sleep she had managed to grab were cascading into her head, so detailed and vivid she was going dizzy, and God, it was stifling in here.

But enough was enough. She couldn't go on like this. It was totally unacceptable. She was a professional. She was here to work. She had to get a grip. And breathe.

'I do,' she said, giving herself a mental shake before stepping forwards into the room and setting her precious cargo on the desk, which unfortunately put her in a position where not only could she see him better, but smell him better too. 'There. Are you impressed?'

Duarte didn't respond. She doubted he'd even heard her. He was wholly focused on the box she'd put in front of him. Staring at it with what looked like barely concealed awe, he leaned forwards, undid the catch and lifted the lid.

Her gaze snagged on his hands as he carefully removed the bottle and slowly twisted it first one way then the other. Strong tanned hands, she noticed, a tingling pulse beginning to throb in the pit of her stomach. Long fingers with a light dusting of dark hair, neat nails. She could envisage them tangled in her hair, on her body, sliding over her skin and—

'Take a seat,' he murmured, popping that little bubble for which she was grateful, yes, *grateful*, not resentful.

Orla sat. She didn't know why. The plan had been to present him with the bottle, remind him of her competence and their deal, at which point he'd unfire her and she'd get back to the business of preparing his estate for the conference. Sitting had not been part of anything. But then, nor had staring and hungering and magnetism, or indeed, weak, wobbly legs.

'Tell me how you did it.'

Right. So normally she didn't divulge her methods any more than she revealed her sources. Both were her currency, and her little black book of notes and contacts was worth a fortune. But in this case, since Duarte was directly impacted, she should probably disclose at least the bare bones of the transaction.

'I made a few phone calls,' she said, determined to ignore his potent allure and remembering instead the events of the last twenty-four hours. 'I tracked one bottle down to Zurich, another to New York and the third to France. This one came from there. I had it flown directly here from Nice and took delivery of it an hour ago.'

He arched one dark, disbelieving eyebrow. 'Just like that?'

Well, no, but there was no way she was going to go into how stressful it had been. How wildly her emotions had oscillated between panic and relief. How slowly the minutes had dragged as she'd waited first for responses to the approaches she'd made and then for the bottle she'd acquired to actually arrive.

So many things could have gone wrong. The plane could have crashed. The box could have been dropped. It could have been stolen en route. Anything. Her nerves had been shredded right up until the moment she had the wine in her hands. But he didn't need to know about the roller coaster of a ride she'd been on today.

'The logistics and insurance took some working out,' she said coolly, as if it hadn't taken every resource she had or wrung her emotionally dry, 'and it took a while to establish that the bottle had been meticulously stored with temperature and humidity control, but essentially, yes.'

Her explanation did nothing to remove the scepticism from his expression. 'So all you had to do was ask, and Antoine Baudelaire simply handed it over?'

If only. 'Not exactly.'

Duarte's brows snapped together, his eyes narrowing a little, and Orla shifted uneasily on her seat because this was where it possibly got a little awkward.

'Monsieur Baudelaire gifted the bottle to his daughter six months ago as a birthday present,' she said, mentally crossing her fingers that he'd be reasonable about the terms that had been agreed. 'It was her I negotiated with. First over the phone, and then over Zoom.'

'His daughter?'

'That's right. Isabelle.'

'What was the price?'

There was no point in pretending there wasn't one. Money hadn't worked. She'd had to get creative. 'She's organising a charity ball around Christmas time,' she said. 'She's been looking for a guest of honour to boost ticket sales and encourage auction donations. She now has one.'

The temperature in the room dropped a couple of degrees and Orla shivered at the thunderous expression now adorning Duarte's perfect features. He sat back and she wanted to lean in to close the distance and capture his scent again, which was completely ridiculous.

'You pimped me out,' he said, a tiny muscle hammering in his jaw.

'I prefer to think of it as a provision of services in exchange for goods.'

'Of course you do.'

His tone was cold, his words were clipped. He was clearly furious, and her heartstrings twanged because

by all accounts he didn't socialise much these days
and the idea of a ball in all its gaiety must be deeply
unappealing. But it was only an evening of his time.
A fair swap, she'd figured, relieved beyond belief to
have secured the bottle with relatively little trouble,
even if it had taken a while to find out what it was
that an heiress who had everything she needed and
an overindulgent father might want.

'Believe me, you got off lightly.'

His face darkened even further. 'In what possible way?'

'She also wanted you to be her date.'

Isabelle had waxed lyrical about Duarte. She'd
never met him but she'd read everything there was to
read about him and pored over every photo. She was
under the impression that she was the one to bring
love back into his life, if only they could meet. However, if Isabelle could see Duarte's expression at this
precise moment, she might have thought differently,
because he now looked appalled as well as angry.

'She can't be much more than a teenager,' he all
but growled.

'She just turned twenty. And you're thirty. I
pointed that out. She eventually saw the better of it.'

It had taken some persuasion, and she'd had to call
on every skill she possessed, but there was no way
Orla was going to agree to *that*. It was one thing of-
fering up his time and his influence, quite another
to act the matchmaker. Her company left that up
to others, and for some reason the mere idea of the

stunning and no doubt perky Isabelle batting her
eyelids at the gorgeous Duarte made her feel like
throwing up.

'Am I supposed to be grateful?'

Quite frankly, yes. The infatuated girl had a crush
on him the size of Portugal. She'd have clung to him
like a limpet and been hard to prise off.

'I could always give the wine back,' she said, with
a quick pointed glance at the wonky bottle that pre-
dated modern glass-making techniques and was
standing on the desk in all its dusty, unassuming
glory. 'All you have to do is say the word.'

The scowl on his face deepened. 'No.'

'OK, then.'

And that, she thought, as a deluge of relief and triumph washed over her, was how it was done.

Orla thought she'd won. Duarte could tell by the
smug satisfaction on her face and the delight dancing in the depths of her eyes, and on a rational level
he knew she deserved her moment of victory. She'd
defied the odds. She'd achieved something that had
always been out of his reach, and he ought to be impressed by what she'd accomplished because, objectively speaking, she was a genius.

On a deeper, more emotional, more turbulent
level, however, the deal she'd struck to secure the
wine sat like a rock on his chest, crushing his lungs
and fogging his head. She'd involved him in her
negotiations and allowed him no say in the mat-

ter. She'd used him to get what she wanted, and the feeling that he'd been manipulated—again—burned through him like acid, spinning him back to a time he'd been taken for a fool, a time he strove to forget.

With the memories of Calysta, her calculations and her volatility descending thick and fast, the fog in his head intensified. Emotion roiled around inside him. Every instinct he possessed was rising up to fight it. The need to regain the upper hand and to shift the balance of power back in his favour hammered through him.

It shouldn't be hard, he assured himself darkly. He held all the cards. Or at least he ought to. He was Orla's client. In a way, he was her boss. Yet he got the strange feeling that bending over backwards to please him simply because he paid her to do so was of little importance to her. Intense relief was woven through the triumph in her expression and it struck him now that there'd been a trace of desperation in her voice when she'd been running after him down the corridor yesterday afternoon, begging him to reconsider firing her. Something that hinted there was more at stake for her than the mere loss of a client.

With the arrogance of someone used to calling the shots and having his every order obeyed, he'd assumed uppermost in her mind would be keeping him happy, but what if all she really cared about was rectifying her mistake?

'Your strategy was a risky one,' he said, the odd, unexpected hit to his pride adding to the turmoil churning around his system and lending a chill to his tone.

'In what way?'

'You're counting on me to hold up your side of the deal.'

As the implication of his words registered, Orla's smile vanished. She went very still and wariness and tension gripped her frame. 'Are you saying you won't?'

And *now* he was back in control, he thought with grim satisfaction. 'I'm simply saying assumptions are unwise.'

Anger sparked in her eyes. 'If you renege on the terms I agreed my reputation will be destroyed.'

'You should have thought of that before you decided to use me.'

'It's one evening of your time and I *did* think of that,' she fired back. 'I read you had integrity, Duarte. I read you played fair. Is that not true?'

It was true, dammit. Just as he fought for his reputation to protect his business against the naysayers, he worked hard for his success and did things by the book. 'It's true.'

'I thought as much,' she said with a curt nod. 'So if I did take a risk it was a calculated one. I considered one evening a small price to pay for something you've been after for years. And yes, I suppose you could refuse to support the ball if you wanted to, but there are things at stake for me here that you couldn't even *begin* to understand.'

So he'd been right about the story. 'Like what?'

'My livelihood for starters.'

Which implied there was more. 'What else?'

'Isn't that enough?' she said, her chin and her guard back up. 'I've worked insanely hard for what I have. Don't destroy me simply because you can.'

And now he was even more intrigued. Why was *she* at risk of destruction, rather than her reputation or her job? What was really behind the offer to complete a challenge she must have known had a stratospheric risk of failure? What made her tick? And, come to think of it, what was she was doing here, seeing to his instructions personally? Who had she been dreaming about while asleep in his bed?

These were questions to which he sorely wanted the answers, he realised with a disconcerting jolt. He had no idea why. But then, nor could he work out why the fact that she'd used him as leverage in her negotiations didn't seem to matter quite so much now as it had a moment ago.

Perhaps the angry energy crackling around her, which gave her a stunning, dazzling glow, had short-circuited his brain. Or perhaps it was because, on reflection, he could see that what Orla had agreed with Isabelle Baudelaire was hardly outrageous. Once upon a time, before he'd met and married Calysta and duty and responsibility had become of primary importance, he'd frequented many a party. More often than not he'd *started* the party. And, as Orla had pointed out, it was only one night and it was for charity, so how tough would it be?

Furthermore, his acceptance of her terms would mean that *their* deal was on and she'd therefore be staying to oversee the preparation of his conference, which would bring benefits beyond mere convenience, because at some point over the last twenty-four hours he'd had to admit to himself that he wanted her. Badly.

What else could account for the change in his behaviour that had occurred the moment she'd mentioned the wine, when these days he *always* stuck to the plan? Why else would he have crashed out on the sofa in this stifling room last night instead of returning to his airy apartment in Porto that benefited from a sea breeze, as he'd intended?

He'd told himself it was simply a more efficient use of his time and better for the planet if he parked the helicopter instead of toing and froing between here and the city of his birth, a distance of some two hundred and fifty kilometres. But that didn't explain the heightened awareness he'd felt all day or the anticipation that had been rocketing through his system ever since he'd received Orla's text asking where they should meet. Or, indeed, the frustration and disappointment that he hadn't run into her today despite making himself wholly available.

No. He wanted to strip off the dress rendered see-through by the evening sun streaming in and tumble her to the sofa so much it was addling his brain, a brain that was already running on empty thanks to a severe lack of sleep. He'd had an uncomfortable night, and not just because his six-foot-three frame was too big for this room's compact two-seater sofa. Enveloped by the warm, velvety darkness, the still silence broken only by the cicadas chirruping in the vines, he'd tossed and turned, his imagination going into overdrive as he'd revisited the events of the day.

What if he'd kissed Orla awake instead of shaking her shoulder? had been the thought rolling around his head even though he was no fairy-tale prince. What if he'd capitalised on the brief flare of desire he'd caught in the depths of her eyes the moment before she'd leapt from the bed as if it were on fire?

His imagination hadn't cared about how inappropriate that would have been. His imagination had embraced hindsight, which recognised that she quite possibly felt the attraction too, and had gone wild, bombarding his head with visions of the two of them setting the sheets alight until he'd had to head to an old disused bathroom to take an ice-cold shower, where finally he'd found relief.

'All right,' he said, his mind teeming with ideas about how he might make the most of the situation that had landed in his lap. 'I'll honour your deal.'

'Thank you,' she said with a brief, confident nod, as if she'd expected his agreement all along. 'And the one between us?'

The one that meant he wouldn't have to find someone else to finish readying the estate, provided the chance to get the answers to the questions he had and offered him the potential to find out if she was as attracted to him as he was to her and, if so, do something about it? It was a no-brainer.

'That one too.'

# CHAPTER FOUR

*Oh, thank God for that,* thought Orla, the tension gripping her body giving way to relief so intense it was almost palpable.

Things had taken an unexpected turn for the worse for a moment back there and the sudden potential reversal of fortune had sent her into an almighty spin, but she'd stayed cool and calm, and disaster had been averted. The mistake she'd made had been fixed. Her job was secure, her reputation was intact and her demons remained buried. Her work here was done. And now, with the adrenalin and stress fast draining away and the monumental effort of controlling her body's wayward response to his taking its toll, all she wanted to do was sleep because she was shattered.

Stifling a yawn, she pushed up on the chair arms and got to her feet, every muscle she possessed aching and sore, and she didn't even pause when he said, 'Where do you think you're going?'

'Bed,' she muttered, envisaging her gorgeously

comfortable room at the hotel and almost weeping with need. 'It's been a very long, very eventful
twenty-four hours.'

'Don't leave just yet. Stay and have a drink with
me.'

Now, that did make her pause mid-turn. Because,
despite her desperation to flee consuming every one
of her brain cells, something about his voice seemed
different. The chill had gone. His tone was smoother,
lighter, less antagonistic and more like that of the
man in her dreams.

Curious, her pulse skipping, she turned back and
glanced down to find that he was looking at her with
focus, with intent, and the tiny hairs on the back of
her neck shot up. At the sight of the decidedly wicked
glint in his eye, and the faint yet devastating smile
curving his mouth, she shivered, and heat pooled
low in her belly.

What was he up to? Why the glint? Why the
smile? Why the abrupt one-eighty personality
change?

She didn't want to know, she told herself firmly.
She was tired and confused and her defences were
weak. She should have ignored him and carried on
with her exit. She shouldn't have allowed her curiosity to get the better of her. She didn't need glints
and shivers. She needed respite from his effect on
her and to recharge her batteries.

'Thank you, but no,' she said, crushing the tiny
yet powerful urge to say yes and indulge her curi-

osity a little while longer because she had a plan to which she intended to stick.

'It doesn't seem right to drink this alone.'

He waved a hand in the direction of the bottle she'd acquired and her eyebrows shot up, shock momentarily wiping out the fatigue and the wariness along with the plan. *'This?'*

He gave a nod. 'Yes.'

'You're planning on *drinking* it?'

'I am.'

For a moment she just stared at him, scarcely able to believe it. Had he lost his mind? Perhaps yesterday's bump to the head had done more damage than had first appeared, because this wasn't just any old bottle of wine. This was special beyond words. Surely it wasn't for drinking.

'But it's over a hundred and fifty years old,' she said, aghast. 'It's worth a quarter of a million dollars. If you drank it, that would be it. History and a fortune blown in a matter of minutes. Shouldn't it be in a museum?'

'It *is* mine, isn't it?' he said reasonably, although she noticed that both the glint and the smile had faded slightly.

'Well, yes, but—'

'I never wanted it simply for the sake of owning it, only to admire it from a distance while it gathered even more dust. I've wanted it for its story, to savour and appreciate it and learn from it. So let Zurich and New York put theirs in a museum. I'll do what I damn well please with mine.'

'Of course,' she said, hastily back-pedalling, since, despite the easy way he'd delivered the explanation, he didn't look at all pleased at having his decision questioned and really she ought not to be antagonising him when she'd only just got her job back. 'It's none of my business what you do with it. But seriously, please save it for your guests at the conference. It would be completely wasted on me. I know nothing about wine. I'm more of a cocktails-with-an-umbrella kind of a girl.'

'Then I'll teach you.'

To her alarm, he surged to his feet in one fluid movement and made for the sideboard on the other side of the room, but she didn't want him to teach her, she thought a bit desperately. She wanted a break from the dizzying breathlessness that she couldn't seem to shake no matter how hard she tried. She wanted space. Sleep. And at some point she really ought to try and figure out why she'd messed up his instructions in the first place. 'What if I don't want to learn?'

'Isn't it your job to see to my every request?'

While the question that wasn't a question hung in the air, Orla narrowed her eyes and shot daggers at his back. Bar the immoral, the illegal or the unethical, it was, damn him, and it occurred to her suddenly that not only was he drop-dead gorgeous, but he was also determined and ruthless and clearly un-used to hearing the word 'no'.

Not that that was remotely relevant at the moment. Why he would want her to share the wine was any-one's guess, but she had the feeling that she was still on somewhat shaky ground and he was the client, which meant that he was right. Within reason, what he wanted, he got. So she'd let him do his spiel, have one quick sip of wine and *then* she'd be off. 'Fine.'

'Excellent. Come and join me.'

Armed now with a decanter and a corkscrew, Du-arte picked up the quarter of a million dollars that he was about to throw down his very tanned, very attractive throat and strode to a seating area where half a dozen glasses stood upside down on a tray in the centre of a coffee table.

Orla eyed the only seating option warily. The sofa wasn't a big one and he'd take up most of it. Perhaps she could drag the chair she'd been sitting on over. But no. It was solidly wooden and impossibly heavy. It wasn't budging, no matter how hard she pulled.

Taking a deep, steadying breath and assuring her-self that it would be fine, that all they were doing was tasting wine, she moved to the sofa and sat down, wedging herself as tightly into the corner as she could. But, as she'd suspected, it wasn't enough. There was just too much of him. He was stealing her air, dizzying her with his proximity and robbing her of her composure, and she had the feeling that alco-hol was only going to make things worse.

Yet she couldn't move. In fact, as she watched him brushing the dust off the neck of the bottle and carefully removing the cap, she wanted to scoot over and lean into him. She wanted to find out exactly how hard and muscled his chest might be. His shirt was unbuttoned at the top to reveal a tantalising wedge of tanned skin and gave her a glimpse of fine dark hair, and her fingers itched to investigate further.

'The grapes that made this wine grew when Queen Victoria was on the British throne,' he said, tilting the decanter and slowly pouring the contents of the bottle into it while she set her jaw and sat on her hands. 'Ulysses S Grant was the US president. Echoes of revolution and Bonaparte still sounded through France. It was a hot, dry summer in Bordeaux that year, a perfect climate for growth and harvest. The vineyard had just been bought by Rothschild. This was the first vintage to be bottled under their ownership. Nothing was mechanised. These grapes were picked by hand and transported by horse and cart. They were trodden by the feet of a hundred locals instead of going into a press as they do nowadays.'

His deep voice was mesmerising. The web he was spinning was lulling her into a sensual trance from which she didn't want to emerge. She was there, in France. She could feel the heat of the sun, smell the dusty earth that mingled with the scent of ripened grapes and snippets of French. She wanted him to tell her more. She wanted him to tell her everything. She could listen to him for hours.

'You paint a vivid picture,' she said, her voice so unusually low and husky that she had to clear her throat to disguise it. 'You have a good imagination.'

He set the bottle down and glanced at her, his eyes dark and glinting with something that made her stomach slowly flip. 'So I've discovered.'

What did *that* mean?

'What if it's turned to vinegar?' she said, forcing herself to focus on the beautiful cut-glass decanter that was now worth a fortune, and not on the hypnotic effect he was having on her.

'It hasn't.'

'How do you know?'

'Smell the cork.'

Twisting round to face her, he held it under her nose and she instinctively inhaled, but all she got was him. Spice, soap, some kind of citrus. An intoxicating combination that muddled her head.

'Delicious,' she murmured, not entirely sure that was a word that could be used to describe the smell of a cork, but then, she wasn't entirely sure either that she actually meant the cork.

'Promising,' he said, and as he turned away to reach forwards and select a couple of glasses she got the strange feeling he wasn't talking entirely about the cork either.

He poured wine into each, watching the flow of

liquid intently as he did so, and then nudged one in her direction. 'Here you go.'

'Do you realise there's around forty thousand dollars' worth of wine in that glass?'

'Forget the money.'

'That's easy for you to say.' It was all very well for aristocratic billionaires. For mere mortals, it was a small fortune. 'Forty thousand dollars in pounds would pay off a considerable chunk of my mortgage.'

'A fair point,' he said with a wry smile that flipped her stomach. 'But this is all about the senses.'

Hmm. Well. She didn't know that her senses would be up to much. They were frazzled, completely overwhelmed by him. He was all she could see…his voice was all she could hear. His scent had permeated every cell of her being and she wanted to touch and taste so badly it was becoming a problem. There wasn't a lot of space left for strawberries or compost.

'What do I do?'

'First you look at it, then you smell it, and finally you taste it.'

God, could he read her mind?

'Hold it against this,' he said, handing her a piece of white paper, which she took with fingers that were irritatingly unsteady. 'Tilt the glass. What do you see?'

Getting a grip, Orla did as he instructed and studied the liquid. 'It's a dark sort of reddish brown in the middle,' she said, her voice thankfully not reflecting any of the chaos going on inside her. 'Paler at the rim.'

'Wine browns as it ages and gets hazier.'

'This is very clear. Is that good?'

'It is. Now level it and swirl it around.'

'What does that do?'

'Two things,' he said, demonstrating in a way that bizarrely made her stomach clench. She valued competence. She appreciated it in others. She'd never found it sexy before, but in him, she did.

'First,' he continued, 'when the liquid touches the side of the glass the alcohol evaporates. What remains—the legs—indicates the viscosity or the degree of sweetness. Secondly, it maximises the surface area and releases the aromas.'

If she'd been in a test and had had to say what came second Orla would have been stuck for an answer. All she could think about now were legs. His legs. The long length of his thighs a foot away from hers and how powerful they might be beneath the denim of his jeans.

'What do you see?'

'No legs,' she said a bit breathlessly as she tore her gaze from his thighs and returned it to the glass. 'This must be very dry.'

'You're a fast learner.'

She'd had to be if she'd wanted to claim her place in her family. She'd worked hard and paid attention. The only area that strategy hadn't proven successful had been in the bedroom. She didn't know why.

She'd tried her damnedest with her ex-fiancé Matt, yet nothing. It was immensely disappointing and insanely frustrating, and for the benefit of her emotional well-being she tried not to dwell on it much. 'I'm good at listening.'

'Let's see what else you're good at,' said Duarte, his eyes dark and glittering. 'Stick your nose in and sniff it.'

It was hardly the sexiest of instructions, yet she had an image of burying her nose into his neck, and longing thudded in the pit of her stomach. His nose, she noticed, was gorgeous. Straight. Perfectly proportioned. Aquiline, even, which wasn't a word she'd ever had cause to use before.

'What do you smell?'

'Cherries,' she said, the aroma of the wine winding through her before gradually separating out into individual strands. 'Something herby. Rosemary maybe. And, weirdly, cheese.'

'You *are* good at this.'

He did the same, only way more expertly than her and for far longer. He considered, muttered something in Portuguese and made some notes on a pad on the table.

'Now taste it,' he said. 'Take a big gulp and swish it around. You should feel the alcohol at the back of your throat.'

'And then?'

'Swallow it and breathe in through your mouth and out through your nose. Note the textures and the

astringency. Then take another gulp. That one you
can either spit out or swallow.'

She would *not* react to that, she told herself firmly.
She wasn't sixteen. But her imagination had other
ideas. Her imagination had her getting up to lock the
door to this room, heading back and then dropping
to her knees before him.

Maybe that bang to the head had done more damage than she'd assumed to her too. She was dizzy
and discombobulated, and when she tried the wine
in the way he'd suggested, knocking it back instead
of spitting it out, she could barely think straight, let
alone take note of its textures.

'What do *you* think of it?' she said, struggling for
control of her thoughts and setting her glass down
before she dropped it.

'It's exceptional. Very vibrant for its age. Long
finish. Impressive.'

'How strong is it?'

'Average. Why?'

'I'm feeling very light-headed.'

'That's unlikely to have anything to do with the
wine,' he said, putting his own glass down before
turning to study her with what looked like concern.
'It could be the heat.'

It was warm in here, that much was true. The sun
at this angle bathed the room in abundant evening
sunshine. But no, it wasn't the heat. That wouldn't account for the throbbing between her legs. It was him.

Her heart was thundering and her temperature

was rocketing, and she could feel it happening inside her again—the strange combination of fire and ice that she'd experienced yesterday when he'd come to an abrupt halt and whipped round in the corridor. Her head was spinning but somehow, in the midst of the chaos, she noticed that he'd gone very still. Very alert. The tension vibrating through him was almost palpable.

As the seconds ticked by the air between them thickened, crackling with electricity. Awareness charged her nerve endings. His gaze dipped to her mouth for a second and her lips tingled. He was so close. All she'd have to do was lean forwards a little and she'd *finally* be able to find out what he felt like, what he tasted like.

'Orla?' he said, his voice very low and gravelly.

'Yes?'

'You need to stop looking at me like that.'

His eyes were blazing and she was dazzled. The rush of adrenalin that was shooting through her was making her feel reckless. 'How am I looking at you?'

'As if you want me to kiss you.'

'I do,' she breathed before she could stop herself, but oh, she *did*. She was going out of her mind. Sex was a problem but kissing would be OK, surely, if he was amenable.

'Well, why didn't you say?' he muttered roughly, clamping one hand to the back of her head to bring her forward and then planting his mouth on hers with a speed that suggested he was very amenable indeed.

She didn't have time or the resources to marvel at that. The inappropriateness of what they were doing didn't cross her mind once. The heat flooding her body and the desire pounding along her veins were wiping her head of rational thought. All she could do was succumb to sensation.

She moaned and wrapped her arms around his neck, and the kiss deepened and intensified. The muscles of his shoulder bunched beneath her fingers as she ran them over him and this time he was the one to groan.

With an urgency that she would have found flattering had she been capable of thought, Duarte disentangled his hands from her hair and moved them to her waist. He lifted and shifted her and then, hardly aware of what was happening, she found herself astride him. He held her hips and tugged her towards him, and when she pressed against him, his erection rubbing her where she so desperately ached for him, she tore her mouth from his and gasped.

But that didn't deter him. He simply set his lips to her neck, lingering on the pulse hammering at its base, while she dropped her head back to give him better access and struggled for breath. With one hand he held her close. He slid the other down her thigh, slipped it beneath the hem of her dress and pushed it up.

Any minute now, she thought dazedly as she burned up with want, her clothes would come off, followed by his, and then there'd be more touching and some body parts would want to be in others and it wouldn't all go wrong for her this time. There'd be no disappointment or despair. There'd be explosions and ecstasy and it would be perfect. More perfect than she could have ever dreamed, and her dreams had been pretty damn good.

But this wasn't a dream, this was reality. The heat and the desire coursing through her were real, which meant that she *could* feel passion, she *wasn't* frigid. She'd always thought she was a failure in the bedroom because she was unable to experience the kind of pleasure she'd heard was possible, but look at what was going on here. Fireworks. Genuine mini-explosions. For the first time ever.

So what if it *hadn't* been her? she thought wildly as he continued to wreak havoc on her skin. She'd only had one lover, her former fiancé, so she had little scope for comparison, but what if the failure had been his? Or maybe it had just been down to simple incompatibility that was nobody's fault.

She hadn't given sex another chance after her engagement had ended because, frankly, if she wasn't going to excel at it, why bother, but could she have missed out on four years of fun and games and even relationships unnecessarily? Need she not have been quite so lonely in all that time?

The questions now ricocheting around her head were huge, breathtaking and utterly overwhelming. On top of the clawing need and delirium, Orla could feel the emotion swelling up inside her, threatening to overspill and quite possibly manifest itself in tears, and that was an outcome she really didn't want to have to explain, so she wrenched herself away and scrambled off him.

'What's wrong?' Duarte muttered hoarsely, breathing hard as he looked at her with eyes that were glazed and burning.

She swallowed down the lump in her throat and tugged at the hem of her dress, as if covering up might provide some kind of defence against the potentially earth-shattering discoveries swirling around her brain. 'I need to go.'

'Do you? Why?'

Because her foundations were rocking and she needed time and space to deal with it. Because the strength of her response to him was scary in its intensity and she was out of her depth here.

'Because this isn't appropriate,' she said desperately, grasping at the only excuse she was willing to give.

'It feels pretty appropriate to me.'

'You're a client.'

'That's irrelevant. I want you,' he said, his eyes dark and compelling. 'Stay.'

'I can't.'

It was one request she couldn't fulfil. Not right now, at least. She couldn't think straight. She didn't know what she was doing. She was totally out of control and it was terrifying.

'Thank you for the wine,' she managed, her head

swimming and her heart pounding. 'See you at the conference.'

And then, before she fell completely apart, she fled.

In something of a stupor Duarte listened to the quick, rhythmic tap of Orla's heels on the stone floor of the *adega* fading away and reflected dazedly that if she thought she wouldn't be seeing him again until the conference in three weeks' time, she could think again. Because a kiss like that did not end there.

It had been hot, wild and wholly unexpected. One minute the conversation had been all about the wine, the next, their gazes had collided and the world had stopped. The hunger on her face and the need he'd seen shimmering in her eyes had lit a rocket beneath his pulse and turned him harder than granite.

Once she'd indicated what she wanted, he hadn't thought twice about abandoning the wine and kissing her. He'd acted purely on instinct, and the minute their mouths had met, desire had crashed through him, flooding every inch of his body in seconds. It still lingered, along with the memory of her in his arms, kissing him back with more heat and passion than he could possibly have imagined, as well as utter bewilderment at how suddenly and swiftly she'd backed off.

Was the strength of his response to the kiss down to the fact that it had been such a long time since he'd wanted anyone? It was impossible to tell. And what had spooked her? Again, he had no idea, although he could sympathise if she'd been caught off guard by the explosive nature of the kiss. The impact of it had hit him like a freight train too.

But for all the new questions racing around his head, one he'd had before had definitely been answered. She wanted him just as much as he wanted her.

So what happened next? he wondered as he leapt to his feet and began to pace around the room, repeatedly criss-crossing the lengthening shadows. Once upon a time, he'd have welcomed the obviously mutual attraction, capitalised on the kiss that had given him a rush he hadn't realised he'd been missing, and pursued Orla without hesitation, without doubt. But he was no longer that man. These days, he was battered and bruised and wary. These days, he had the responsibility for a billion-euro business to keep him occupied.

And yet, it wasn't as if he was after a relationship. Thanks to his marriage, from which he still hadn't recovered, he was never having one of those again. In fact, his blood turned to ice at the mere *thought* of it. Love was manipulative and commitment was a prison. And he didn't just have his own experience to base his opinions on. His parents' unpleasant and messy divorce had proved that long ago.

But sex with someone with whom he shared the kind of chemistry that led to unbelievable pleasure? The one-or-two-nights-only sort of thing he'd fa-

voured before he'd married? That he could handle.
That would be perfect.

He felt more alive, more energised this evening
than he had in months, and he wasn't about to give
that up. So he'd put in the groundwork. He'd allay
any fears or doubts Orla might have. Seduction had
once come to him as naturally as breathing and it
wouldn't take too much effort to brush off the dust
and fire up his skills. He'd have her in his bed in no
time. So, contrary to her parting shot, she wouldn't
be seeing him in three weeks' time. She'd be seeing
him tomorrow.

# CHAPTER FIVE

WHAT A NIGHT.

Stifling a yawn and wishing she didn't feel quite so bleary-eyed, Orla climbed into the car and fired up the engine to drive the seven kilometres that lay between her hotel and Duarte's estate.

To say she hadn't slept well was an understatement. Two fitful hours, from three to five, was all she'd managed, and that was on top of the sleepless, stressful night before. She was therefore running on empty, which didn't bode particularly well for a day during which she needed all her wits about her, but at least she was fortified with coffee and the conviction that nothing was going to go wrong.

There was no reason it should, she assured herself as she turned out of the hotel's entrance and onto the road. She was meeting the housekeeping team she'd hired in an hour. She'd confirmed the time and printed off a copy of the instructions she'd already emailed to them, and all other arrangements were on track.

Of course, it would help enormously if she could stop thinking about what had happened yesterday evening. The memories of the kiss she and Duarte had shared had tormented her for most of the night, rendering her so hot and bothered that she'd wondered if she was coming down with something.

The heat and skill of his mouth moving so insistently against hers... The rock-hard muscles of his chest flexing beneath her hands... The glazed look in his eyes and the faint flush slashing across his cheekbones and the heady satisfaction of knowing she'd caused both... And then the abrupt, mortifying way it had ended.

She hadn't had the chance to contemplate the notion that the mediocre sex she'd experienced to date might not be her fault after all or regret the time she'd potentially wasted. She hadn't had the wherewithal to find out how the venue mix-up could have happened. Distressingly, she hadn't had the head space for anything other than the actual kiss itself.

But at least today she'd be so busy concentrating on the job she was here to do she wouldn't have time to dwell on these things. It wasn't as if she and Duarte's paths were going to cross. She'd made it very clear she didn't expect to see him until the conference and there was no earthly reason why someone like him would bother himself with anything as mundane as housekeeping. He had a billion-euro global wine business to run and presumably multiple demands on his time. So there'd be no awkward moments involving stuttering conversation and fierce blushing. No gazing at his mouth and remembering. There was nothing to worry about at all.

Orla swung off the road and onto the wide, sandy drive that led to the Quinta, the awe rippling through her as fresh as it had been when she'd rushed over the day before yesterday, shortly after her initial, monumental mistake had come to light.

As conference venues went, this one was spectacular. The house had been built on the north bank of the Douro at the beginning of the eighteenth century, the year the estate was bought by an ancestor of Duarte's who'd travelled from the UK to try his hand at making port. Against a cloudless azure sky the white walls of the three-storey building sparkled in the early morning sunshine beneath a terracotta tiled roof. Green shutters were open at the ground-floor windows that stretched out either side of the huge oak front door, and at those above on the next floors up.

Behind the facade, the original building had gradually tripled in size and been regularly modernised. It now boasted ten en-suite bedrooms, countless reception rooms, a dining room that could seat fifty, and a ballroom, which was where the meetings would be taking place. At the rear, the courtyard that was decorated with jewel-coloured mosaics featured a fountain in the shape of a cherub holding aloft a bunch of grapes. And beyond that, a vine-covered pergola stood over a wide stone patio that ran the length of the house and had stunning views of the terraces.

Over the years, the success of that intrepid eighteenth-century winemaker had led to the expansion of the business and the acquisition of further estates, and almost all of the winemaking had since moved to Porto. But, given its size and idyllic setting, this magnificent building had been used for entertaining for the past three centuries and still was.

Quite honestly, Orla still couldn't work out how she'd got it so wrong. The house she'd originally and incorrectly identified as the venue for the conference was lovely—now that it wasn't a complete tip—but it wasn't a patch on this.

She should have questioned the keys that didn't fit, she thought for what had to be the thousandth time. She should have paid more attention to the odd curious glance she'd received over the ten days or so, which she'd attributed to miscommunication as a result of her poor attempts at Portuguese. She shouldn't have been so confident she knew what she was doing that she hadn't triple-checked the instructions.

However, now wasn't the time for unfathomable conundrums. Now was the time to focus on the day ahead, a day free from distractions and lapses in concentration, a day devoid of slip-ups.

Everything was going to go brilliantly, she reminded herself as she pulled up at a wing of the house to the rear, the tradesmen's entrance, got out and bent to retrieve her satchel from the back seat.

She had her lists and the order of play. She knew what she was doing, and, more importantly, she knew what everyone else was doing. Everything was under control.

'*Bom dia.*'

At the sound of the deep voice somewhere behind her, Orla jumped, narrowly avoiding hitting her head on the roof of the car, and whirled round. Her heart gave a great crash against her ribs and then began to race. Duarte was striding her way, his gaze fixed on her, a faint smile hovering at his mouth.

*Oh, no,* she thought, her heart sinking as the memory of last night's kiss, the wantonness of her response and the way she'd been all over him instantly slammed into her head and flooded her cheeks with heat.

This was bad.

Very bad.

What was he doing here? Why wasn't he doing something brilliant with wine? What had happened to their paths absolutely not crossing? So much for a day free from distraction and loss of focus. Ten seconds in his vicinity and already panic was beginning to flutter inside her. Already she was on edge and wired in a way that had nothing to do with the copious amounts of caffeine she'd consumed earlier. But what could she do? She could hardly order him to leave. It was his estate.

'Good morning,' she replied, hitching her satchel over her shoulder, locking the car and deciding that denial and professionalism while she figured out a way to get rid of him were the way forward here.

'Did you sleep well?'

No. She hadn't. She'd slept appallingly. 'Perfectly well, thank you,' she said, setting off for the back door. 'You?'

'Barely a wink,' he said as he fell into step beside her. 'You kept me up for hours. Literally.'

Her pulse thudded, her mouth went dry and she very nearly stumbled. Why would he say that? How did he expect her to respond? Was she supposed to apologise?

She'd never been in this situation before, working in such physical proximity with a client. She didn't know how to handle it. But she was pretty sure that if he'd decided to start flirting with her it wasn't going to help at all. It wasn't helping much that despite his allegedly rough night he still looked unfairly gorgeous. No washed-out skin or dark, saggy bags under the eyes for him. *He* hadn't had to slather on the concealer or paper over the cracks.

'Did you finish the wine?' she asked as she walked through the door he held open and into the beautifully cool house.

'I lost the taste for it.'

What a frivolous waste.

Heroically resisting the urge to roll her eyes, Orla started down the long flagstone-floored passageway that led to the kitchen and tried to ignore how near he was. The passageway was as wide as the Douro.

There really was no need for his arm to keep brushing against hers. Every time it did, tiny shivers scampered through her body. She even felt them in her toes, for goodness' sake.

'So what are you doing here?' she asked, aiming for politeness and trying not to let her frustration show.

'I thought I could lend a hand.'

With what? What did he think he was going to do? Make up a bed? Did he even know how to? Judging by the mess she'd found at his house, assuming it had been caused by him, it didn't seem likely.

'I have everything under control,' she said, deciding that on balance it was probably better not to be thinking about beds, hands or, in fact, any other body part of his. 'I'm meeting the housekeeping team here in,' she glanced at her watch, 'half an hour.'

'Local?'

'Yes.'

'I'll help translate.'

'The team leader speaks excellent English.' Honestly. Did he really think she wouldn't have thought of that? 'You pay a hefty fee not to have to bother with any of this, Duarte,' she said pointedly while just about managing to retain her smile. 'You really don't need to stick around.'

'I want to.'

But why?

Unless…

Her eyes narrowed as an unwelcome thought occurred to her. 'Do you think I'm going to screw up again?'

'Not at all. But you can answer one question for me,' he said, striding ahead of her into the vast kitchen and taking up a position against an expansive stretch of work surface.

Orla made for the enormous wooden table that stood in the middle of the room and had three centuries of food preparation scored into its surface and sat down. 'What do you want to know?'

'Why are *you* here, seeing to things personally?'

Well, at least *that* was a question she could answer. 'I was let down at the last minute by the team I'd put in place to carry out your instructions,' she said with an inward wince as she laid her satchel on the table and opened the flap. 'They're the best. I use them all the time. Fly them across continents. But they got struck down by a bug. All of them at the same time. It's never happened before. I spent two days trying to fix up a replacement but then decided it would be quicker and simpler to do it myself.'

It had been a frantic, stressful time and in hindsight, *that* was probably why she'd misread his email.

'But why are *you* here?' she asked, wondering if it had really been that simple. 'You weren't due back for another three weeks.'

'I had business in the States. It wrapped up early.'

Which in some ways had been a good thing, she had to admit grudgingly. While his happening upon her taking a nap hadn't been ideal, imagine if her mistake hadn't been uncovered until the day of the conference. There wouldn't have been time to fix things. He'd have been even more furious, and justifiably so. She felt faint at the mere thought of it.

'So when you think about it,' he mused with a nonchalance she didn't trust for a second, 'neither of us is meant to be here. Fate, wouldn't you say?'

She would say nothing of the sort. 'I don't believe in Fate.'

'No, I don't imagine you do,' he said with a quick, dazzling grin. 'You're too practical. But mistakes aside, you're dedicated.'

'*One* mistake;' she corrected, determinedly blinking away the dazzle and reminding herself that practical wasn't boring, practical was good. 'Which is being rectified. And it's my job.'

'Which you love.'

'I do,' she agreed as she began removing her laptop and notebooks from her bag. 'Who wouldn't? It involves opulence. Outlandish, unforgettable, once-in-a-lifetime experiences. VIP events. Unimaginable excess and extravagance.'

It also required stellar organisation, infinite skill when it came to persuasion and negotiating, and the ability to think on her feet. Every single day demanded and expected more from her than the day before, and she was one of the best. Usually.

'Recently, I arranged an engagement proposal on an iceberg,' she said, as much to remind herself of her competence as to prove it to him. 'Once, a cli-

ent wanted to have a private dinner in front of the
Mona Lisa.'

'I ought to up my game.'

Orla reached for her clipboard and thought that
Duarte's game was quite high enough. They spoke
at least twice a month. His requests ranged from arranging private jets to reserving tables at impossible-
to-book restaurants and much more besides, and they
were frequent. While most of what he wanted hov-
ered at the bottom of the outrageousness scale, last
year he'd asked her to recreate a perfume long since
out of production for his mother as a birthday present. That had been a challenge. 'You keep me busy.'

'I could keep you busier.'

Orla froze in the middle of attaching her lists to
the clipboard and shot him a startled glance. What
did he mean by that? She couldn't work it out. His
words were innocent enough but the way he was
looking at her was anything but. He was sort of
*smouldering* and quite suddenly she was finding it
a struggle to breathe. He'd gone very still and his
gaze had dropped to her mouth, which went bone-
dry, and oh, dear God, was he thinking about last
night? Was he planning a repeat?

She was so hopeless at this, she thought desperately, her heart thundering while a wave of heat
crashed over her. But *this* shouldn't even be happening. She shouldn't be burning up with the urge to
get to her feet, throw herself into his arms and take

up where they'd left off. She shouldn't want him to spread her out over the table and feast on her.

The speed and ease with which he could make her lose control was confusing and terrifying. It was as if there were wicked forces at play, luring her into the unknown, over which she had zero control, and if there was one thing she hated, it was that.

But now cool-headed logic battled against hot, mad desire, and she feared it was losing—

And then, relief.

Blessed, blessed relief.

'I think I hear a van.'

By the end of the day, Orla could stand it no longer. Her nerves were in tatters and her stomach was in knots.

As she'd hoped, the work side of things was going splendidly. The house had buzzed with activity. The housekeeping team she'd organised was as efficient and excellent as she'd been assured. Rooms were in the process of being cleaned and laundry pressed. Anything that could be polished shone, and vacuum cleaners had hummed throughout the building all day. Her mistake was well underway to becoming history and her satisfaction on that front was deep.

But, as she'd feared, Duarte was proving to be a menace. While she'd been handing out instructions and emphasising priorities, he'd donned a tool belt. Subsequently, everywhere she'd turned, up he popped, sometimes with a hammer, other times with a screwdriver, and once, when a basin tap was discovered to be leaking, with a wrench. At one point she hadn't seen him for an hour and had dared to hope that he'd gone for good, but unfortunately he'd returned with lunch. For everyone.

There seemed to be no end to the man's talents and it was driving her nuts. She couldn't stop thinking about the smouldering. The tool belt, combined with olive combat shorts and a white polo shirt that hugged his muscles and highlighted his Portuguese heritage, was such a good look on him, she could hardly tear her eyes away. His smile, which he wielded frequently and lethally, laid waste to her reason every time she caught sight of it. So far today she'd knocked over a vase, temporarily mislaid three of her precious lists and spent a good fifteen minutes she could ill afford to spare gazing out of a top-floor window at where he was methodically clearing leaves from the pool, having waved aside protests from the team of gardeners handling the outdoors.

She didn't like it. Any of it. Not the loss of focus, not the weakening of her resolve, and she particularly hated the sinking sensation that if things continued in this vein, a serious slip-up was only a matter of time.

She couldn't allow that to happen, she thought grimly as she stood at the back door and watched the convoy of vans carry off the three dozen housekeeping staff for the night. She was striving for excellence here and for that she needed to stay on the ball. Right now, not only was she *not* on the ball, she wasn't even anywhere near it. She felt as if she was walking a tightrope. One wobble and she'd tumble to the ground, where her insecurities lay waiting to pounce.

So enough was enough. Forget the fact that Duarte was a client who ought to be kept happy at all times. Forget that this was his house. She couldn't carry on like this. She had to find him and get rid of him. Whatever it took.

Beside the pool, Duarte unbuckled the tool belt and dumped it on a lounger. He emptied his pockets of his keys, wallet and phone, then stripped off his polo shirt. After removing his belt and adding it to the mounting pile of belongings, he dived into the cool, fresh water with relish.

The day had been surprisingly enjoyable and unexpectedly revelatory, he reflected as he began to swim lengths, the heat in his body and the tension in his muscles easing with every powerful stroke. He'd already come to the conclusion that, despite initial impressions, Orla was exceptionally capable. Why else would she be joint CEO of her company and how else could she have acquired the elusive wine? But who'd have thought competence would be such a turn-on? She issued crystal-clear instructions, could mentally turn on a sixpence and solved problems with head-spinning speed. She was like a highly efficient, well-oiled dynamo. She demanded excellence and got it, and the longer he'd watched her in action the more insistent the desire drumming through him became.

Whether or not she still wanted him, however, was as clear as mud. She'd spent most of the day trying to avoid him. He strode into a room and she marched out. He'd brought her lunch—since the oat bars she snacked on were hardly the kind of sustenance needed for a long day's work—and she'd responded not with appreciation, as one might have expected, but with a huff of barely concealed disappointment. When avoidance had been impossible, she'd opted for ice-cool professionalism, as if she hadn't melted in his arms and kissed him so passionately last night.

Her frosty attitude towards him didn't bode all that well for his intention to entice her into his bed, Duarte had to admit as he turned and started a length underwater, but he had no intention of giving up. She wasn't the only one with goals. Once he set his mind to something, nothing swayed him. So he'd stick to the plan—perhaps even ramping it up—and she'd succumb soon enough. The women he'd wanted in the past generally had and he didn't see why Orla would be any different.

Coming up for air, he caught sight of her marching across the grass towards him. He swam to the side of the pool, his pulse hammering with an intensity that could have been caused by the exercise but more likely was because of her, and rested his arms on the tiled edge just as she drew to a stop right in front of him.

'Duarte,' she said in the clipped tone he'd become used to over the last twelve or so hours and which, perversely, fanned the embers of desire and sent it streaking through his veins like fire.

'Orla,' he murmured, letting his eyes drift from her fine ankles, up her shapely legs and over her shorts and T-shirt, which were close-fitting enough to make him want to get his hands on the skin beneath and trace her shape.

'We need to talk.'

Oh, dear. That sounded serious. He'd never been a fan of 'talking'. At least, not about anything that mattered, anything that might hurt. Shortly after the deaths of first his son and later his wife, his mother had tentatively suggested therapy. Beleaguered by unimaginable grief and excoriating guilt, he'd instantly shut that conversation down and sensibly she hadn't revisited it. What had happened was his fault, he knew, and he didn't deserve to work through it and come out the other side. He deserved to burn in hell.

'What about?' he drawled, pushing the unwelcome memories down and burying them deep.

'You. More specifically, this…' she waved a hand around '…*situation*.'

Interesting.

What precise situation did she mean?

Assuring himself he could easily deflect the con-

versation if it headed down a path he'd rather not follow and somewhat relieved that the idea of 'talking'
had deflated his desire when his shorts now clung
to him like a second skin, Duarte heaved himself
out of the pool. He gave himself a shake and strode
over to the lounger. He reached for his polo shirt and
used it first to rub his hair dry and then to blot the
water from his chest. When he was done, he stalked
over to the table that could seat twelve and draped it
over the back of one chair before dropping himself
into another.

'I'm all yours,' he said, leaning back and stretching out to let the evening sun do its thing.

When Orla didn't respond he glanced up at her.
She looked dazed. Flushed. She swayed for a second
and he briefly wondered if she was about to pass out.
Today had been scorching and long. It wasn't beyond
the realms of possibility.

'I'm sorry?' she stammered.

'You wanted to talk? About me and a situation.'

She blinked and snapped to. 'Yes. That's right.
I do.'

'Fire away.'

'Okay.' She cleared her throat and tucked a lock of
wavy golden hair that had escaped her ponytail behind her ear. 'Yes. Good. I just wanted to say thank
you for your help today. It was…appreciated.'

She didn't sound as if it was. The moment's hesitation suggested his presence here today had been any-

thing but appreciated, which was intriguing. 'You're welcome.'

'However, there's no need for you to be here to-morrow.'

'It's no trouble.'

'Really. I wouldn't want to put you out.'

'You won't.'

'I'm sure you must have somewhere better to be.'

She was wrong. For once, he had time on his hands, and while there was always something in the business that required his attention, he could afford a few days off to focus on this latest project. He had the feeling that it would be more than worth it. 'I don't.'

Her stunning eyes flashed with annoyance. 'Well, you can't stay here.'

'Why not?'

'You're getting in the way and putting me off my stride.'

'Your stride looks fine to me,' he said, his gaze dropping to her long legs and lingering.

'You're being deliberately obtuse.'

'Then clarify it for me.'

She let out a sigh of exasperation and threw up her hands in what looked like defeat. 'I can't con-centrate while you're around,' she said hotly. 'You're too distracting. I need to be able to do my job to the best of my ability and you're preventing me from doing that.'

Her admission jolted through him like lightning, electrifying every nerve ending he possessed. So she *was* affected by him. She was just remarkably adept at hiding how she felt. It was surprisingly satisfying to know. 'I bother you.'

She gave a nod, her jaw tight, as if she was loath to have to admit it. 'Yes.'

'And yet you're still brilliant.'

'I am,' she agreed. 'And I've worked very hard to be. But I won't be brilliant if I keep dropping things and losing lists. You're making me do that. You mess with my head. All day I've been on tenterhooks waiting for some disaster to happen because I'm not paying enough attention, and I can't have it.'

'I think you're overestimating my powers.'

'You couldn't possibly understand.'

'So explain.'

'I have to be in control,' she said, glowering down at him and shoving her hands in the back pockets of her shorts, which did interesting things to her chest. 'I need everything to be perfect. All the time. I can't accept second best. It's just not in me.'

'You're a high achiever,' he replied with a nod. 'I get that. So am I.'

She shook her head. 'It's more than that. For high achievers, the goal is important but mainly it's about the journey. My older brother and younger sister are classic examples of that, so I should know. Nothing fazes them. If something goes wrong they dust themselves off and pick themselves up. They see it as a lesson learned. For me, it's all about the goal, which I have to reach no matter what. It's not about the journey. I couldn't care less about that. I just want results. Failure sends me into a spin. I sink into a pit of self-doubt and despair and it's not a good place for me to be. Ergo, I can't fail.'

So that was why she'd been so desperate to get her job back after he'd fired her. As he'd suspected, rather disappointingly, he found, it had had nothing to do with him. 'That's a lot of pressure.'

'You have no idea,' she muttered vehemently. 'It's fine if I stay on track. Not so much if I don't. Which is what's happening here.'

'I make you panic?'

'Yes.'

'Because I distract you.'

She scowled. 'What do you want? A medal?'

No. He just wanted her. She looked like a goddess standing there in the sun, her hair gleaming beneath the rays, fire in her eyes. A frustrated and annoyed goddess, it was true, but she was magnificent none the less, and desire hammered hard in the pit of his stomach.

'I want you to admit you want me as much as I want you,' he said, focusing every drop of his attention on her so he didn't miss a thing. 'I want you to admit you can't stop thinking about our kiss.'

'Fine,' she snapped, clearly at the end of her tether. 'I *am* attracted to you. I *can't* stop thinking about our kiss. It kept me awake all last night. It's been plaguing me all day. It's—*you're*—driving me nuts.'

'Then I have the perfect solution.'

She frowned at him for one long moment, her expression wary and her body tense. 'What is it?'

'Sleep with me.'

# CHAPTER SIX

FOR A SPLIT SECOND, Orla thought she'd misheard. That she'd been so dazzled by the sight of him—his broad, muscled chest, tanned, bare and glistening in the evening sunshine—she'd lost her ability to think.

And to be honest, briefly, she had. Duarte had hauled himself out of the pool and she'd practically combusted on the spot. All she'd been able to do was stare and drool. When he'd lowered his gaze from her face to her legs just now, leisurely perusing the bits in between, she'd been so transfixed that she hadn't even been able to take a breath, let alone summon up a protest at his blatant and outrageous scrutiny.

Her brain had clearly been starved of oxygen by that because she hadn't meant to confess how strongly he affected her. 'Whatever it took' had not meant exposing her vulnerabilities to a man who already wielded far too much power over her. It had not meant admitting to an aspect of her personality that she'd been told, by a therapist she'd seen once when her engagement ended and she spiralled into a pit of self-doubt and hopelessness, was a flaw.

Could she have been subconsciously hoping that he'd sympathise and retreat? If she had—and frankly, she had no idea why that would have been the case when she barely knew him—it had badly backfired. All she'd done was give him ammunition. However, what was said was said and it was too late to take any of it back, and in any case the conversation had taken an unexpected turn.

Surely he couldn't have said what she thought he'd said. And if he *had*, then surely he had to be joking. But he didn't look as though he was joking. His expression was filled with dark, dangerous intent and his voice had dropped an octave, just as it had the evening before when he'd asked her to stay.

'You've lost your mind,' she managed once she'd unglued her tongue from the roof of her mouth and regained the power of speech.

'Not in the slightest,' he said with a cool, even tone that she would have envied had there been space for it amongst all the heat and desire crashing around inside her. 'By your own admission you're distracted because you're attracted to me. That attraction won't go away just because I do. It's too powerful. It will linger. Fester. Swell until it grows out of all proportion, and then you really *will* be distracted. Then you really *will* make mistakes.'

He didn't sound quite so cool now. He sounded

like he knew what he was talking about. 'Are you speaking from experience?'

The shrug he gave was careless, but she could practically see the shutters slamming down over his eyes and his guard shooting up, which suggested she was right. Who? When? How fascinating.

'If you want your concentration back, you need to get what's throwing it off course out of your system,' he continued, interestingly leaving her question unanswered. 'Demystify it and it loses its power. We want each other. You're driving me as mad as I apparently drive you. So let's do something about it. Scratch the itch and it goes away.'

Seriously?

No matter how certain Duarte sounded, to Orla that didn't make any sense. Eradicate the attraction by indulging it? She might not have much knowledge on the subject but she didn't think it worked like that. What if it didn't go away? What if it got stronger? *More* distracting? And if sleeping with Duarte was so good that she ended up with further itches that needed scratching, how on earth would *that* help?

'What if it doesn't?' she said, her head fogging at the thought of feeling even more for him than she already did.

'That's never been my experience. Once is generally enough.'

For him, maybe, but what about the women he took to bed? What about her? 'I'm really not sure it's a good idea,' she said with staggering under-statement.

'Incredible sex is always a good idea.'

Well, yes, perhaps in *theory*, but she wouldn't know, and the whole idea of sleeping with him felt recklessly dangerous. Not only could she find herself way out of her depth, but also she really didn't fancy making a fool of herself, which was what could well happen if hell froze over and she did throw caution to the wind to take Duarte up on his suggestion.

According to the gossip columns, he'd bedded hundreds of women in the years preceding his marriage. Beautiful women. Experienced women. Imagine if something started between *them* and she got it all wrong. Imagine if her inability to truly enjoy herself in bed hadn't been down to her ex or simple incompatibility but was in fact because of something in *her*. What if the sparks and heat she felt in his vicinity didn't last? What if his effect on her somehow disappeared beneath the pressure to perform, to excel? The humiliation would be unbearable. She'd never be able to work with him again. She wouldn't even be able to look him in the eye.

But on the other hand, insisted a little voice in her head that was becoming increasingly loud, what if it didn't? What if she was overthinking this and quite possibly missing out on not only the opportunity to turn a failure into a success but also some apparently pretty scorching sex in the meantime?

Didn't she owe it to herself to see if she couldn't

rectify the situation that had been bugging her for years? She was nearly thirty. How much longer was she going to put it off? And perhaps Duarte was right and just the once *was* the way to get it out of her system. He had vastly more experience than she did, so maybe chemistry *did* work like that. Out of sight, out of mind hadn't exactly been a success. Look at how her night had panned out.

Something had to give here, and she had to at least *try* and find out what she was capable of, she thought, the possibility of it beginning to drum through her. She'd never experienced lust before—which presumably was what all this was—and who knew when the next opportunity might come along? Surely the effect he had on her—so wild and intense—had to mean that anything between them would be better than good.

Deep down, she longed to know whether the reality could live up to her dreams, and what was the worst that could happen? That it didn't? That she felt nothing and had to fake it? Well, that wouldn't be a problem. She excelled at *that*. Her ex hadn't guessed for a moment that her panting and moaning was calculated and strategic rather than spontaneous and instinctive, and if it came to that, nor would Duarte.

'Incredible is a bold claim,' she said, her mouth as dry as the desert and her heart thundering like a steam train.

His dark gaze glittered in the setting sun. 'Incredible is a guarantee.'

Was it? He seemed so sure. Did she dare? To grab the chance to right a wrong and experience some allegedly hot sex with the most attractive man she'd ever met, a man who astonishingly seemed to want her as much as she wanted him, and wasn't really a professional conflict of interest? Why, yes. Despite the potential for failure, apparently she did. 'All right.'

For a big man Duarte moved with impressive speed. Barely before she'd had time to blink he was up and off the seat and closing the distance between them with single-minded intent. He stopped an inch in front of her, planted a hand on the small of her back and drew her in.

'Here?' she managed breathlessly, as her senses swam and her skin beneath his palm burned. 'Now?'

'Do you have a problem with that?'

The heat swirling in the depths of his eyes as he stared down at her took her breath away and her thoughts spun for a second. Ludicrous thoughts, such as when had she last examined her bikini line? What underwear was she wearing? Did it matter? Would he even notice? Given the focus and intensity with which he was looking at her, she doubted he would notice a thousand champagne bottles popping simultaneously behind him. And her body was all right. She kept herself in shape and depilated. It would probably be best to strike while the iron was hot and just get on with it, before she talked herself out of it.

'No,' she said huskily, lowering her gaze to his mouth and feeling a surge of longing so overwhelming she didn't quite know what to do with it. 'No problem at all.'

She put her hands on his bare chest and his hold on her tightened and then he was kissing her, hot and hard. Her heart thundered and fire licked along her veins. She slid her hands up, over warm skin and taut muscles, skimming over his shoulders, until her fingers came into contact with his thick, soft hair. She held his head and he pulled her hips to his, and when she felt the steely length of his erection against her she gasped.

Taking advantage of the break in kissing, Duarte, breathing heavily, removed her T-shirt and, ah, yes, now she remembered. Her underwear was practical and sturdy rather than sexy and feminine, cotton not lace, designed for comfort while at work in the heat. Not that he appeared to mind. He seemed more intent on getting her horizontal. He manoeuvred her round and down and then she was lying back on a double sun lounger, free to ogle him as he reached for his wallet and extracted what she presumed was a condom.

God, he was gorgeous. And he clearly knew his way around a female body. But what would someone like him—former international playboy, looks of a god—expect? Presumably incredible sex required incredible input on her part, but what ought she to be doing? His skills were evidently extensive, while hers were very much limited, and how on earth was she supposed to get an A-plus when she hadn't even revised for the test?

She'd close her eyes and trust her instinct, she told herself firmly. She'd stop thinking and focus on feeling. She was a fast learner. She'd pick up the clues quickly enough. There'd be no problem.

Duarte joined her on the lounger and lowered his mouth to hers, kissing her deeply while she closed her eyes and moaned. Her hand went to the nape of his neck and his moved to her breast. She arched her back, pressing herself against him harder, seeking the tingles she'd experienced the night before, but they remained annoyingly elusive.

Why was that? she wondered frustratedly as he rubbed his thumb over her nipple and she sighed with what she hoped he'd interpret as ecstasy. What was she doing wrong? And, come to think of it, where was the reason-wrecking heat and all-consuming need off to? She could feel it dissipating and she tried to recapture it but to no avail, and no, no, no, no, *no*. This wasn't meant to be happening. She wasn't meant to be panicking that she was going to mess it up. She was meant to be doing *this* and doing it well.

Duarte ran his hand down her body, and in anxious desperation Orla writhed in a way designed to indicate passion, in an attempt to reignite it inside her, but it was as if she were watching the proceedings from somewhere far, far away, and she wanted to cry with despair and frustration.

So much for getting the craziness out of her system. Right now, it wasn't even *in* her system. With all her overthinking, she'd killed the mood. For her at least. But she needn't kill it for him, and who knew, maybe his desire for her would be strong enough for both of them?

Panting hard and frantically hoping to relocate the need that had been tormenting her for days but was now stubbornly absent, she trailed her fingers down his back and round to the button of his shorts. She started undoing it, feeling the hard length of his impressive erection beneath her hand, when he suddenly put his hand over hers and stilled her movements.

'What are you doing?' she said huskily, looking up at him with what she hoped was an encouragingly seductive smile. 'Why are you stopping?'

His eyes were dark and glittering, and a deep frown creased his forehead. 'This isn't doing it for you, is it?'

What? Damn. Why couldn't he have believed her pants and moans, the way her ex had? Why did he have to notice she was struggling to focus? He wasn't helping by putting a halt to things. Couldn't he see that?

'Just carry on,' she murmured, trying to shake his hand off hers so she could continue undoing his fly. 'It'll be fine.'

He stared down at her, as if unable to believe what he was hearing. *'Fine?'*

Oh, dear. Now she'd offended him. 'I meant, I'm sure it'll be incredible,' she said with a batting of her eyelids and a twist of her hips. 'There'll be explosions and ecstasy. Whatever. It's all good.' Or it would be if she could get out of her head. Probably.

'It is far from all good,' Duarte said grimly, disentangling himself from her, sitting up and moving to the edge of the lounger.

Orla missed his heat immediately and inwardly railed at her inadequacy. There really was no hope for her. 'I'm sorry,' she said, feeling quietly mortified and very exposed.

He looked at her, his eyes stormy and every line of his body rigid. 'You never have to apologise for changing your mind.'

'I haven't changed my mind,' she said, keen to make that clear despite the hopelessness she could feel descending. 'That's not it at all.'

'Then what is it?'

'I started thinking about excellence and expectations and got a bit sidetracked.'

His eyebrows shot up. *'Sidetracked?'*

'Well, yes. You must have slept with lots of women. I, on the other hand, have only slept with one man, not very successfully. You're way more experienced than I am. I have no tricks.'

He retrieved her T-shirt and handed it to her and she put it back on, feeling a little chilly now. So much for hoping her lack of success at sex might have been the fault of her ex or incompatibility. It was clearly neither. It was her. There was something wrong with her.

'What are you doing tomorrow?'

Orla swallowed hard. Right. He was obviously no longer interested and it was back to business. 'The same as today, I expect,' she said, determined not to care. Making sure everything went smoothly and avoiding him, most likely. Only instead of being distracted by memories of the kiss on his sofa, she'd be trying not to think of what had happened here.

'Take the day off.'

What? 'I can't.'

'Everyone here knows what they're doing, right?'

'Well, yes…' Apart from her obviously. She didn't have a clue.

'And you have a phone in case of emergencies.'

'I do, but—'

'Then you can take the day off.'

Why was he so insistent? Why wasn't he simply marching off and going in search of someone who *did* know what they were doing? 'What for?'

'Further research into excellence and expectations,' he said, his deep, hot gaze holding hers so she couldn't look away even if she'd wanted to. 'And tricks.'

Oh.

*Oh.*

Maybe he was still interested. Orla's pulse skipped a beat and then began to race but she ignored it because she knew now that that translated into precisely nothing. So what would be the point in pursuing things? It would be a disaster again and there was only so much humiliation a person could take.

'There's no need for that,' she said thickly, her throat tight with disappointment and regret.

'There's every need for that,' he countered. 'You're not the only one with goals, Orla. I'm not accustomed to mediocrity either, especially when it comes to sex. So take the day off.'

Orla considered taking the day off a mistake. Duarte knew this because he'd picked her up from her hotel half an hour ago, after she'd done what needed to be done at the Quinta, and she'd already mentioned it half a dozen times. She'd cited professionalism. She'd muttered something about there being a problem with the tablecloths. She'd repeatedly asked herself what she thought she was doing. Out loud.

He, on the other hand, considered it anything other than a mistake. He'd never had a woman in his arms simply going through the motions. He didn't like it. Either his skills were rustier than he'd imagined or Orla required a different approach. Whichever it was, he wanted to get to the bottom of what had sidetracked her. His desire for her was so strong that if something wasn't done about it soon he could suffer permanent damage. His male pride was wounded and demanded satisfaction, and it was more than three long years since he'd last slept with anyone.

So if overthinking was her problem then he had

to get inside her head and disrupt from within. He sensed there was a volcano bubbling beneath her surface that needed erupting. He also had the intriguing feeling that the sex she'd previously had, *not very successfully*, was involved, and that, therefore, also merited investigation.

'Where are you taking me?'

With any luck, by the end of the day, to heaven and back. 'The river.'

'Why?'

'Because while you're here you should see more of the local area than just the Quinta. It's beautiful off the beaten track. Nature at its most excellent.' Not to mention far away from work and reality and ideal for his purposes. 'And speaking of excellence, where does your need for it come from?'

'You don't waste time.'

He took his eyes off the road for a split second and cast her a quick glance to find that she was looking at him both shrewdly and suspiciously. 'I don't see the point,' he said, totally unperturbed by this. Orla was skittish and wary and easily spooked by matters of a carnal nature, but she was also trapped in a moving car. He could afford to be direct. 'My badly bruised ego demands answers.'

'I'm a lost cause.'

'How do you know? We've barely even begun.'

'Experience.'

Ah.

'Also, were you not there last night?'

'I was very much there,' he said, remembering how soft and warm she'd been in his arms, how divine she'd smelled and tasted, and feeling a pulse of heat low in his pelvis. 'Even if you weren't.'

'I was to begin with, before getting sidetracked.'

Duarte crushed the pressing yet wildly inappropriate urge to pull over and find out if she still felt that good and reminded himself of his plan to find out what made her tick. 'So back to my question...'

'I'm the middle of three siblings,' she said on a sigh. 'My older sister is an opera singer. A contralto. She's with the Met and lives in New York. My younger brother plays rugby for England. My parents were generally to be found either at a concert hall or on a touchline somewhere. There wasn't a lot of time left for me, you know?'

'No,' he said. 'I wouldn't know. I'm an only child.'

'So you got all the attention.'

He caught a note of wistfulness in her voice, guessed that she was imagining a happy family unit that was all hearts and flowers, and the cynic in him felt compelled to burst that particular bubble.

'Not exactly,' he said flatly, his hands flexing on the steering wheel. 'My parents divorced when I was twelve. Acrimoniously. They were so busy hurling insults at each other, there wasn't a whole lot of time for me either.'

That hung between them for a moment, then she said softly, 'I didn't know that. I'm sorry.'

'No need,' he replied, really not needing her pity.

'It's been eighteen years and they're civil to each other now. We all rub along well enough. But for a decade I did end up seeking attention elsewhere. Everywhere, actually.'

'You found it. In spades.'

'I did.' And he hadn't regretted a minute of it. Until he'd met Calysta and lost his head.

'I had to work for mine,' she said, putting a stop to his turbulent thoughts before they could head down that dark and twisted path. 'And my only option was school. I studied hard, all the time, making sure I came top of the class every term and acing every test.'

'Did it work?'

'It did. The first time I got a hundred per cent in a maths exam my parents took us all out for a meal to celebrate and *I* was allowed to choose the restaurant. I was eight and it was the best moment of my life, so I didn't stop. I carried on aiming for the top and claiming what snippets of attention I could. Luckily, I really enjoyed studying.'

'What about friends?'

'What friends?' she deadpanned.

She had high expectations of herself. She probably had high expectations of others that were hard to live up to. As he'd thought, the pressure she put on herself must be immense. 'How did you become joint CEO of Hamilton Garrett?'

'I didn't bother with university,' she said. 'There was nothing I was interested in apart from organising and making everything just so, and there isn't a degree for that. After I left school I became an executive assistant at a bank and worked my way up until I became the aide de camp for the bank's president. I left there to start at what was then plain old Hamilton Concierge Services. My aim was always the top and after a lot of blood, sweat and tears I got there last year.'

'Impressive.'

'Just focused and determined.'

'Is there anything you *don't* excel in?'

'Not much. But then, I tend to steer clear of things I know I won't be good at.'

'Such as?'

'Opera singing and rugby,' she said drily.

'That's it?'

A pause. 'There may be other stuff,' she said, hedging in a way that piqued his curiosity.

'Like what?'

'Just stuff.'

'Sex?'

It was an educated guess, based on the last couple of nights, but he could feel her blush from all the way over here and he knew he was right. She was satisfyingly easy to read.

'It's complicated.'

'So it would seem.'

'Anyway,' she said briskly. 'I think that's quite enough about me. What about you? The business press sings your praises almost weekly. You're said to have the Midas touch when it comes to wine and sales and things, and you're good at fixing sinks and fetching lunch. You pursue excellence, too.'

'But not at the expense of all else.' He had friends. He didn't fear failure. Not professionally, at least. On a personal level, it was a different matter altogether. He'd failed his wife and son so badly the guilt and regret still burned through him like boiling oil. But he learned from his mistakes. It wouldn't happen again. Ever.

'You think it's a flaw,' she said, a touch defensively.

'Don't you?'

'No. Why on earth would it be? Why wouldn't you want to be and do the best you can? Besides, the pursuit of perfection keeps me on an even keel and I like feeling good about myself.'

Was it the only thing that made her feel good about herself? That didn't sound healthy, but then, what did he know? He was hardly a role model in matters of self-worth. He'd spent a decade wreaking havoc across Europe trying to find his. Thanks to his unforgivable role in the deaths of Arturo and Calysta, it still remained elusive.

'But you are not alone in thinking it's a problem,' she continued, refocusing his attention before it tumbled down that rabbit hole of pain and guilt. 'I once went to a therapist who suggested the same thing.'

'Why did you need a therapist?'

'I didn't. My mother arranged it and I was in too

bad a place to summon up the energy to refuse. My engagement had ended and I was wallowing in a vat of self-doubt and despondency.'

'But not heartbreak?' he said, astonished to hear she'd been engaged when by her own admission she didn't even have friends.

'Well, yes, that too, obviously.'

'What happened?'

'We discovered we weren't suited. My expectations of him were too high apparently, which again I don't see as a problem, even if he did. I mean, what's wrong with wanting and expecting things from people, including the best?'

'Nothing.'

'Quite.'

'As long as what you want and expect isn't beyond what they can give, of course.'

Orla didn't seem to have a response to that. As he swung the Land Rover off the road and onto a bumpy track, Duarte glanced over to see she was looking at him shrewdly, a faint frown creasing her forehead. The memory of their conversation about attraction, the moment she'd asked him if he was speaking from experience in particular, flew into his head and his chest tightened as if gripped by a vice. She was astute. All this talk about therapy and relationship expectations was making him uneasy. If she decided to turn the conversation back to him, asking the kind of questions he'd been asking her, probing into the deeply personal, the roiling of his stomach would get worse and that was hardly the plan for today.

So it was a good thing, then, that, as he pulled up beneath the wide-spreading branches of an acacia tree, they'd reached their destination.

'We're here.'

# CHAPTER SEVEN

'HERE' WAS A deserted bend in a stretch of the river that flowed close to the border with Spain but still within the district of Bragança. On both banks, terraces planted with vines were carved into the steep hills that descended to the shore. Just beyond the spot where Duarte had stopped, a golden sandy beach protected by a dense forest shimmered in the hot midday sun. It was secluded and beautiful, quiet and tranquil, and couldn't have reflected Orla's inner state less.

She was just so confused, she thought despairingly, hopping down from the Land Rover and seeking distance and air by wandering down to the shore. By Duarte and his effect on her, but also, more pertinently, by herself. She didn't understand what she was doing. She knew she shouldn't have accepted his invitation to spend the day with him. She had myriad excuses to decline—principally work and the mortification of the evening before—yet she'd found a counter argument to every single one of them.

Why had she done that?

Could it be because she simply wanted to find out more about him? Their interactions over the phone and email were naturally all about him and what he needed from her, but here, so far, the conversation had been all about her. Adept at deflection, he'd largely remained an enigma. So had she accepted it to correct a perceived imbalance that had her constantly on the back foot? Or really, did she just burn with the need to uncover the stories that lay behind the shadows that occasionally flitted across his expression and the guarded wariness that she sometimes caught in his gaze?

If it was the latter, she reflected, lifting her hand to shield her eyes as she gazed at the stunning panoramic view, she wasn't doing a very good job of it, because apart from the brief yet illuminating glimpse he'd given her into his upbringing, the conversation on the way here had hardly corrected any imbalance. On the contrary, it had tipped the scales further in his direction.

What on earth made her want to tell Duarte everything about herself? Why had she brought up the subject of her ex? His way of plain speaking must have rubbed off on her, but whatever had prodded her to mention it, she wished she hadn't. His comment about not expecting more than someone was able to give had stuck in her mind. Was that what she'd done with Matt? Had her expectations been unfairly high? While breaking off their engagement shortly after he'd been made redundant, he'd called her draining, unsupportive and impossible to please. At the time, she'd believed that if he couldn't match up, if he wasn't good enough to get another job, that was his problem, but maybe it wasn't that simple.

Adding to the general chaos filling her head was the suspicion that she'd agreed to today because, despite the disaster of last night, she actually wanted a conversation with Duarte about expectations and tricks. She wanted to know what his goals were, particularly with regards to her. It was entirely possible that deep down, against all the odds, despite all the evidence, she still had hope. Her pulse had skipped a beat when he'd pulled up outside her hotel. Sitting next to him as he drove her here had made her stomach churn and she'd felt as if she couldn't breathe even though the Land Rover had no roof and oxygen abounded.

It was madness, none of it made any sense, and, for someone who always knew what she was doing and where she was going, this flip-flopping of thoughts, the loss of control and her irrational behaviour was a worrying state of affairs. The most sensible, safest thing to do, therefore, would be to tell him she wanted to go back, but that ship had sailed because she didn't.

With a sigh of exasperated helplessness, Orla turned round and walked back to the Land Rover, where Duarte was heaving a cool box out of the boot with impressive ease. Perhaps she'd find some kind of comfort by attempting to rebalance the scales of personal information. Probing into the tragedy of his family might be a step too far, but there were plenty of other things she wanted to know. If *she* was the one asking the questions for a change, perhaps she'd be able to claw back some sense of control.

'How did you find this place?'

'It's part of the estate,' he said, handing her a blanket and taking the cool box and a basket to a flat, grassy, shady spot at the edge of the beach. 'A well-kept secret passed down the generations.'

Part of the estate? Just how big was it? They'd driven for nearly an hour to get here, the road winding up through hill after hill before dropping into the valley. It had to be vast. 'It's spectacular.'

'It's the perfect place for a picnic.'

And what else? Seduction? Who else had he brought here? Lovers? His wife? 'Do you come here often?'

'Not for years. As a university student I brought a girlfriend here once. I haven't been back since.'

With inexplicable relief, Orla laid out the blanket. Duarte dropped to his knees, opened the cool box and began setting out the food, a mouthwatering selection of cold meats and cheeses, tomatoes, olives and rolls. Then from the basket he produced a clear bottle half filled with ruby-coloured liquid, and two glasses.

'What's that?'

'Our wine.'

*Their* wine? Hmm. She sat down and frowned. 'Is it still drinkable?'

'Should be.' He poured a measure into each glass and handed her one. 'I've been meaning to say thank you.'

'You're welcome.'

'I was impressed.'

It was odd how her pulse gave a little kick at that. 'You didn't look it.'

'You'd succeeded where I'd failed,' he said with a wry smile. 'My pride may have been dented.'

Was that what it had been? With his confidence, he didn't seem the type, and when she recalled how icy he'd become on hearing how she'd acquired it she had the feeling there'd been more to it. 'Is your pride really that fragile?'

'As an eggshell. Hence why we're here.'

Right. Last night. Goals of his own. Research into expectations and tricks… And what had they been discussing again? Ah, yes. The wine.

'Why didn't you finish it the other night?' she asked, at least ten degrees warmer than she had been a moment before.

'I don't drink alone.'

'Why not? Too great a temptation?'

He gave a slight shrug. 'Something like that.'

Not something like that, Orla decided. Or at least not *just* something like that. Could he have been responsible for the terrible mess she'd found at the house ten days ago? Could drowning his sorrows have been the way he'd handled the deaths of his wife and child? Had he been there, done that? It did seem to be the obvious explanation, and rumour had it he had disappeared for two whole months. However, that was a question she *wasn't* going to ask. That was way too personal.

And in any case *this* glass of wine was making her think of the kiss in his office-slash-sitting room. Of legs. Of tasting and touching and an overwhelming of the senses. She'd let her head get the better of her too then, she thought with a sigh that she stifled with a sip of the wine that was indeed as delicious now as it had been a couple of days ago. Truly, she was her own worst enemy.

With a 'Help yourself' Duarte handed her a plate, and waited for her to take her pick of the smorgasbord before filling his own. Orla sat back and crossed her legs and tried not to ogle as he stretched out on his side and propped himself up on an elbow.

'This is delicious,' she said, nibbling on a chicken leg, then wiping her fingers on a napkin and contemplating what to sample next.

'The cafe in the village is superb.'

'Do you cook?'

It was hardly the most exciting of conversational topics but she was finding it hard to keep her mind off his hands. She could recall them on her body and, despite the heat of the sun, shivers were skating down her spine. But she'd been here before and wasn't the definition of madness doing something over and over again, expecting different results?

'Occasionally,' he said, breaking open a roll and stuffing it with slices of *presunto*. 'I eat out a lot.'

'For work?'

'Yes. Before I took over as CEO, I was in charge of PR and marketing. It involved a lot of wining and dining.'

'I bet you were good at that.'

He flashed her a quick, dazzling grin. 'I was very good at that.'

He was very good at everything. Except, she rather thought, answering some of her questions truthfully.

'So how did you become CEO?' she asked, popping a piece of soft, creamy cheese into her mouth and almost groaning with delight as the flavour burst on her tongue.

'My father wanted to retire,' he said smoothly. 'The timing was right.'

'Any charges of nepotism?'

'Some.'

'Disproved?'

'I would hope so.'

'I signed you up shortly after.'

He regarded her thoughtfully. 'You're good with dates.'

'I have to be. For my job. So where do you live?' she asked before he could start questioning her about dates of a different kind, which, in her case, were non-existent. He'd once described Casa do São Romão as his home, and maybe it had been for a while, but no one had been living there for a long time.

'I have an apartment in Porto.'

'That's a long way.'

'It is,' he agreed with a nod.

'Do you go there every evening and return every morning?'

'No. I've been staying here. At the Casa. Where I first found you.'

She spun back to the moment this had all begun, remembering how hostile and grim-faced he'd been back then—was it really only four days ago?—and her heart skipped a beat. Was he sleeping in the bed she'd slept in? On the same sheets? For some reason that felt incredibly intimate and her cheeks heated.

'What's the story there?' she asked distractedly, trying to get the fluster and the blush she could feel hitting her face under control.

'What do you mean?'

Oh, no.

Her heart gave a lurch and her gaze flew to his. He'd gone very still, the lazy smile nowhere to be seen, his guard sky high, and she wished she could retract the question because she genuinely hadn't meant to ask. But now she had, she wasn't about to take it back. The curiosity had been killing her. 'The house was a total mess.'

His eyes shadowed for a moment. 'Yes.'

'What happened?'

'The cleaner quit.'

She didn't believe that for a moment. 'You should have asked me to find you another.'

'It must have slipped my mind.'

No, it hadn't. She doubted it had even crossed his mind, and part of her wanted to press him on it, but his jaw was rigid, his eyes were dark and his expression was filled with...yes, *anguish*.

Her heart turned over and her throat tightened, and she ruthlessly quelled the questions spinning round her head. She couldn't make it worse for him. This time of year had to be awful enough anyway. His son had been stillborn in early May. His wife had died six weeks later. Three years ago next fortnight, in fact. On both occasions her company had sent flowers, a wholly inadequate gesture, she'd thought at the time, if conventionally appropriate.

'I believe we were going to have a discussion about tricks,' she said, now deeply regretting the fact that she'd invaded his privacy and desperately seeking a way to lighten the mood.

As she'd hoped, the anguish faded and a gleam lit the dark, stormy depths of his eyes, and some of the tension gripping her muscles eased.

'I'm intrigued by the ones you think I know.'

'Well, obviously I don't have details,' she said, putting her plate to one side, her appetite gone. 'But I've read the gossip. You've slept with a lot of women.'

'You shouldn't believe everything you read.'

'Do you deny it?'

'No.'

'How many?'

'I've never kept count.'

'That many? You *must* have tricks.'

'I don't,' he said simply. 'What I do have is instinct. I watch, listen and learn. There's no manual and there are no expectations other than that everyone has a great time.'

Everyone? How many women did he have at once? God, the sun really was scorching today. 'Do you really think that the only way to get rid of attraction is by giving in to it?'

'Yes.'

He sounded adamant, but surely his wife had to have been the exception. Presumably in marriage, the continuation of attraction was a bonus rather a hindrance. But then, what did she know? She was hardly an expert. She'd once planned to marry a man to whom she'd only very tepidly been attracted, which boggled the mind because if she compared the effect Matt had had on her with that of Duarte, well, there *was* no comparison.

'As I mentioned,' she said, determinedly ignoring the unacceptable longing to know more about his marriage when she'd already probed far too much, 'my experience is limited.'

He arched one dark eyebrow. 'The ex-fiancé?'

'Yes. And it wasn't all that great.'

'How long were you engaged?'

'Six months. We dated for a year before that.'

'You implied you had no friends.'

Well, no, she didn't. At least, none that she'd call good and none that lasted. Her hours were long, longer since she'd bought into the business and half of it was now her responsibility. She didn't have much time for socialising. And that was fine. 'I work a lot.'

'So how did you meet?'

'Via a dating app.'

She'd been twenty-four and lonely, not to mention still a virgin, thanks to her determination to outperform all her targets at work. She'd wanted to rectify that, since it had somehow felt like failure. Matt had seemed perfect, as driven professionally and personally as she was, and the future had looked so golden she'd forced herself to simply accept the fact that the sex was lukewarm at best.

'How did he propose? On an iceberg?'

As if. 'Over breakfast one morning. He's a tax accountant. He said it would make good fiscal sense to pool our resources, which in hindsight, explains a lot.'

'When did it end?'

'Four years ago. A long time, I will admit,' she said in response to his arch of an eyebrow, 'but crappy sex isn't hard to miss, especially when it was probably all my fault anyway.'

'How the hell would it be your fault?'

'I think I might be frigid.'

'You are far from frigid,' he said, his gaze drifting over her before settling on her mouth. 'You just need to think less and trust in the chemistry. Ours is outstanding, by the way, and that's unusual.'

'What a waste.'

'You also probably need to be in control.'

She stared at him, the ground tilting beneath her for a moment, and said, 'Do you think so?' even as a tiny voice in her head went, Well, *duh*.

'You said so yourself.'

'I was talking about work.'

'Why would it be different in other areas?'

Hmm. Perhaps it wouldn't. She'd never analysed control as an issue before. But, thinking about it, events beyond her control were generally the ones that sent her into a panic, which was why she tried so hard to mitigate them. So maybe he had a point.

'And in light of that,' he continued, his gaze lifting to hers, the heat blazing in his eyes hitting her like a punch to the gut, 'I should tell you that you can do anything you want to me whenever you want.'

Her mouth went dry and her breath hitched. 'Seriously?'

'Completely. You'd be one hundred per cent in charge. You could decide what you like and what you don't like and you could stop any time.'

'Would that make a difference?'

'You'll only know if you try. Give yourself instructions. Give *me* instructions. You're good at that.'

She was. And it was tempting because she wanted

to experience rockets going off and bone-melting bliss. But then, there was the night of the kiss and yesterday, and the possibility that history would repeat itself, at which point she'd have to catch the next plane home with her tail between her legs and hand his account to a colleague, which wasn't an attractive prospect.

'You don't take instructions,' she said.

'No, I don't. But for you, I'm prepared to make an exception.'

'Why?'

'Because I want you. You're stunning and sexy as hell. And passionate, beneath the surface. It seems a shame to let all that go to waste. And I like you.'

For a moment, Orla was speechless. She was too busy gazing at him and melting like butter in the sun to be able to even think straight. He thought her stunning? He liked her? Had he taken another bang to the head?

'But what if you don't like what I do?' she said eventually.

'I very much doubt that would be possible,' he said, his voice low and so very certain. 'There are no rules. Just do what comes naturally.'

Oh, to have his confidence. But she'd never done anything naturally. She didn't trust in instinct. She studied and planned and practised until everything she did was perfect. She proofread her emails three times before hitting send. When she had to give a presentation she didn't leave anything to the last minute, oh, no. She had it ready weeks in advance, all the better to practise it, practise it and practise it some more. She just didn't understand how instinct— uncontrollable and unpredictable—could be more reliable than careful, considered preparation.

But maybe this wasn't something that could be studied. There was no test, at least, not that she knew of. And what was she going to do? Embrace celibacy, live half a life, in case she continued to fail? That sounded like failure of a different kind. And rather cowardly. So could she change the habit of a lifetime and switch from study to instinct?

Perhaps there was only one way to find out.

Her heart was by now crashing against her ribs so hard she feared one might crack, but Orla drummed up every drop of courage she possessed and said, 'Lie back.'

A muscle in Duarte's jaw jumped and an unholy glint lit his rapidly darkening eyes. 'See?' he said, a wicked grin curving his mouth as he slowly rolled over, using his elbows to prop himself up. 'I told you that you were good at giving orders.'

'Don't talk. I need to concentrate on doing what comes naturally.'

'Ironic.'

'Shh.'

If he wasn't going to be quiet she was going to have to put his mouth to an alternative use. Would that be a good place to start? The right place?

No.

There was no right place. She'd start wherever she

wanted to start. And right now, she wanted to explore his body, in detail and at length. Determinedly silencing the hyper-critical voice in her head that was desperate to analyse what she was doing and assess her performance, Orla moved across the blanket, avoiding the remnants of lunch, and knelt beside him, stretched out before her like her own personal banquet.

With her breath in her throat, she leaned forwards and began undoing the buttons of his shirt, taking her time, savouring every inch of gorgeous tanned skin that her movements exposed. But it was awkward at this angle. She felt like a doctor examining a patient—not the ideal scenario to be envisaging—so she shifted, yanked up her skirt, and in one smooth movement she was sitting astride him, and ah, yes, this was better. From here, she could put her hands on his shoulders, and with his help remove the shirt altogether.

As she began to trace the muscles of his chest and then lower, of his abdomen, he tensed and let out a long hiss, and when she lifted her gaze to his face she saw that his eyes were dark and stormy and his jaw was rigid.

He wanted her. A lot. She could feel the hard steel of his erection pressed against her soft centre, and suddenly, unexpectedly, a rush of liquid heat poured through her and settled low in her pelvis. Her head spun and her pulse raced, but she wasn't going to analyse it. She wasn't going to think about anything. Instead, she was going to kiss him.

Bending forwards and training her gaze on his mouth, Orla planted her hands on the blanket and lowered her head. Her lips settled on his and she tentatively slid her tongue between them to meet his. As she explored him, slowly and thoroughly, her eyes fluttered shut and sparks danced in her head. Her senses took over and it wasn't even a conscious decision that she'd had to make. She was far too drugged for that. He tasted of rich wine and delicious wickedness. His spicy, masculine scent wound through her, intoxicating her further.

She could feel his restraint as he kissed her back, in the rigidity of his body and the curling of his hands into fists at his sides. To know how strongly she was affecting him gave her the biggest of kicks and the confidence to tear her mouth from his and move it along his jaw. The feel of his stubble against her skin made her shiver and his breathing was harsh in her ear. When her mouth closed over the pulse hammering at the base of his throat, he actually growled.

Badly in need of air, Orla drew back dazedly, genuinely panting, and looked down, and somehow, *instinctively* maybe, her hands had made their way to his chest. His heart was thundering beneath her palms, almost as hard and fast as hers, and oh, look, now they were sliding down over hot skin and a light dusting of hair that narrowed down and disappeared beneath the waistband of his shorts.

She was burning up. Her T-shirt was too tight. She was struggling to breathe, and without thought, without a care, she whipped it off and tossed it to one side. Her bra—lacy today, as if subconsciously she'd *known* that this was a possibility—followed a moment later, leaving her bare from the waist up and exposed to his gaze. But the brush of a breeze made no difference to her temperature, not when Duarte was looking at her with such blazing hunger.

'You're killing me,' he said roughly.

He sounded tortured and for a split-second Orla wondered whether she was doing something wrong, but there *was* no right or wrong, she reminded herself firmly. There was just heat and desire, and to her giddy delight she was still feeling it all.

But she wanted more. Much more.

'Touch me,' she murmured, her voice scratchy and low.

With one swift move, Duarte shifted her down and pushed himself up, one arm sliding round her back to hold her in place. Orla was still catching her breath when his other hand landed on her waist, but she nevertheless felt the sizzle across her skin, as if she'd been branded.

'More,' she gasped, wrapping her hands round his neck and sinking her fingers into his hair while he obliged her by sliding his hand up her side to her breast.

He cupped her there, stroking her feverish flesh, and oh, it was so very different to the night before. Tingles were spreading through her entire body, tiny sparks of electricity that she felt from the top of her head to the ends of her toes and made her tremble. She groaned, she couldn't help it, and this time there was nothing fake or forced about it. This time it had risen up from somewhere deep within her.

She was dizzy with longing. Able to focus on nothing but the sight of his large, tanned hands moving over her skin and the burn they left in their wake. She was growing increasingly desperate to find out what she was capable of, to do something to ease the gnawing ache intensifying inside her. Breathing hard, she reached down. With trembling fingers and a banging heart, she undid his belt then grappled with his fly. Duarte shifted so that she could shove his shorts and underpants down, and then he was in her hand, velvety hot and as hard as iron.

But running her fingers over him wasn't enough. She wanted him in her mouth, to taste him, to find out if he liked that, *how* he liked that, so she planted a hand on his chest and pushed him back. He let out a soft gasp of surprise, but when she scooted down his body and closed her mouth over him, doing to him exactly what she wanted to do, his gasps became harsher, more ragged, and shudders racked his powerful body.

Nature was marvellous, instinct was wonderful, and oh, he *did* like that. He liked every lick, every stroke. And so did she, she liked it a lot, but the claw-ing ache was relentless now and she badly wanted him inside her. She lifted her head and looked at him. His eyes were dark and dazed and his jaw was clenched, tension gripping every muscle of his body.

'Condom?' she managed, her pulse hammering and her breath coming in sharp, shallow pants.

'Basket.'

The roughness of his voice, almost a growl, scraped over her nerve endings and, about to expire with need, Orla reached over and found it.

'I hope you don't think I'm using you,' she said shakily as she ripped the packet open.

'You aren't but I couldn't care less if you were,' he said through gritted teeth, taking the condom and applying it with impressively swift efficiency while she rid herself of her knickers.

Catching her lower lip with her teeth, she lifted her hips and sank down onto him, her breath hitching at the incredible feel of him, so big and deep inside her. She leaned forwards to kiss him, her hands on his shoulders for support, and began to move. She couldn't help herself. It was as if her body had a mind of its own and she was merely along for the ride.

And what a ride it was becoming. Her blood was on fire. Her bones were melting. Their kisses were generating enough electricity to power a small coun-try and with every wild roll of her hips, sensation blazed through her.

So this was the result when you let things happen naturally, she thought dazedly, as the pressure inside her grew. This was what it was like to moan and groan and sigh without intending to.

Duarte clamped one hand on the small of her back and the other to the back of her neck, pressing her more tightly against him and angling her head to deepen their kisses, as if able to read what she needed and taking care of it. And she found she was all right with that. She was all right with everything. More than all right, in fact.

Her movements were becoming wilder, more uncontrollable. Kissing was impossible and she was unbearably hot. Her body didn't feel like her own. It was being driven by a need that defied analysis—huge, overwhelming, breathtaking. She ached all over, the tension filling her agonising. Her heart was thundering, the pressure was building and she was racing in the direction of something that was barrelling towards her.

And then somewhere in the recesses of her brain, she was aware of Duarte reaching round and pressing his fingers against her with mind-blowing accuracy, and suddenly, with a cry she just couldn't contain, she shattered into a million scorching pieces. Wave after wave of pleasure crashed over her, so intensely she saw stars. Pure ecstasy flooded her entire body and she found she was shaking all over, fighting for breath, for sanity, and convulsing around him.

And when he thrust up one last time, impossibly hard and deep, a great groan tearing from his throat

as he pulsed into her over and over again, triggering
tiny aftershocks of delight, she knew that it had been
perfect. Wonderfully, gloriously, perfect.

# CHAPTER EIGHT

UTTERLY SPENT, HIS mind blown and his body bone-less, Duarte flopped back, taking Orla, sweat-slicked and limp, with him. He was breathing hard and reel-ing, scarcely able to believe what had just happened. When he'd suggested she take the initiative and run with it, he'd expected she would need a lot more persuasion. He'd anticipated something resembling a slow burn. Instead, he'd encountered a wildfire.

He couldn't remember the last time he'd come across such enthusiasm. Or experienced such exqui-site agony. He'd never had any trouble relinquishing control when it came to sex, but how he'd managed not to touch her at first he had no idea. The thorough-ness with which she'd explored him… The torture she'd subjected him to… When her mouth had closed over him he'd nearly jumped out of his skin. When his orgasm had hit, he'd almost passed out.

Orla carefully lifted herself off him, making him wince slightly as she did so, and immediately he missed the soft, warm weight of her body. He was filled with the urge to pull her back into his arms and relight the fire that burned between them, because, despite the fact that he hadn't yet got his breath back from the last quarter of an hour, he wanted more. A lot more.

Which, he thought with a disconcerting jolt as he turned away to deal with the condom with surprisingly shaky hands, was…unexpected.

He hadn't been lying when he'd told Orla that in his pre-marriage experience, one night had generally been enough to satisfy any desire he'd felt. He'd been easily bored and had enjoyed variety, constantly seeking the attention he'd craved in new people. But apparently he'd changed in more ways than one in the last few years, because not only could he take or leave attention these days, he was far from bored with Orla and the thought of variety made him want to recoil in disgust.

Which meant what? What did he want from her? More of this, absolutely, but nothing permanent, that was for sure. So something temporary, then. Sex for as long as she was here, perhaps. That could work. In fact, that would be ideal, because it would both assuage his rampant desire for her until it burned out altogether and provide a much-needed distraction. The anniversary of his wife's death, which never failed to challenge his ability to keep the crushing pain of betrayal and the overwhelming guilt under control, was rapidly approaching. An affair with Orla would be infinitely preferable to seeking solace at the bottom of a bottle, which was how he'd handled both the immediate aftermath of the tragedy and the anniversaries of the last two years.

Wanting more with her was no cause for concern, he assured himself as he rolled back to face her and propped himself up on his elbow while the plan in his head solidified. It wasn't as if he wouldn't be able to send her on her way when it was over.

What *was*, potentially, a worry was whether she'd be on board with the idea. She'd agreed to a one-time thing. That might have been enough for her, a tick in a box, a failure overcome. The control was still in her hands—she could easily turn him down—and that put him faintly on edge, but he'd just have to persuade her to see things his way because this felt like a win-win opportunity to him and he was not going to pass it up.

'So you were right,' she said huskily, still sounding a little breathless.

'About what?'

'I'm not frigid.'

She certainly wasn't. She was the opposite. She was as hot as hell. Volcanic, in fact, just as he'd imagined. So why on earth, when she pursued excellence on all fronts, had she'd chosen to marry a man who'd never been able to tap that? 'There really isn't anything you don't excel at, is there?'

She stretched languidly, tousled and flushed, half naked and stunning, and gave him a wide, satisfied grin. 'Not a lot, no. And anyway, back at you.'

She was wrong. He did not excel at everything. Far from it. He let his emotions cloud his judgement. He had a tendency towards self-absorption. He failed to protect those for whom he was responsible, and the consequences of these weaknesses of his were devastating and irreversible.

But that wasn't what this afternoon was about, so he shoved to one side the memories and the guilt, focusing instead on the gorgeous, pliant woman beside him, and said, 'Just imagine what we could do with more practice.'

'More practice?' Orla echoed softly, staring at him wide-eyed as surprise and delight mingled with the lingering traces of pleasure. 'I thought that once was generally enough.'

'So did I,' Duarte murmured, his gaze dark and hot as it slowly and thoroughly roamed over her. 'But I was wrong.'

'So what are you suggesting?'

'An affair. For the next three weeks, until the conference is over and we both leave. I'm not after a relationship, Orla. I have neither the time nor the inclination. But I do want you and I want more of this. So what do you think?'

Quite frankly, Orla thought that she'd never been so relieved to hear anything in her life. Even Isabelle Baudelaire's *'Oui, bien sûr'* in response to her request for the wine paled in comparison.

Because what had just happened had been the

most intense experience of her existence, and she knew with absolute certainty that once wasn't going to be nearly enough. How could it be when it had been so unbelievably good? She wanted him again, right now, and how that was possible when she could still barely feel her toes she had no idea.

That he didn't want a relationship was fine with her. Why would he? He'd had the perfect marriage, which had been tragically cut short. His wife was irreplaceable. Peerless, even. Who could ever compete with a ghost like that?

But she didn't want a relationship either. One was quite enough, and the thought of another, which would inevitably end in deep disappointment and endless self-recrimination, was enough to bring her out in hives, and she too didn't have the time.

But she did want more sex with him, and whether or not itches were scratched or multiplied she didn't care. She ought to do more research. What did once prove anyway? And she needed to know just how excellent she could be, he could be, they could be together. She wouldn't get distracted. She excelled at multitasking. It was only three weeks. It would be hot, intense and fun, and when the conference was over she'd walk away with happy memories and no regrets.

'An affair it is.'

For Orla, the next few fabulous days were revelatory, in both expected and unexpected ways. Having handed her the key to unlock the secret to spectacular sex, Duarte had unleashed a devil she hadn't even known she'd been guarding. The first time she'd experienced the heady heights of earth-shattering bliss by the river had just been the start of it. He'd taken it upon himself to prove to her exactly how much pleasure her body could endure, which had turned out to be a *lot*, and by the end of the day she'd been completely drained, so lethargic, her body so boneless, she'd barely been able to move.

Control was a powerful thing, she'd realised as she'd lain there in the glow of the afternoon sun, catching her breath yet again, stars dancing in her head. But so was having the kind of confidence that meant you could temporarily let it go. And that was what he'd given her—confidence—over and over again.

The realisation that she was capable of excellent sex, that she'd finally overcome an obstacle that had been bothering her for years, had been so overwhelming that at one point during the afternoon she'd had to take a moment by going for a wander alone along the shore.

Perhaps she should take more risks, she'd thought, gently kicking at the cool water lapping at her feet. Perhaps she shouldn't simply avoid things she didn't think she'd be any good at. Because maybe, just maybe, she'd turn out to be the opposite. And look what could happen when she *did* take a risk. Yes, there was always the possibility of failure, but should she *not* fail, the results could be astounding.

From that afternoon on, when she wasn't over-seeing progress at the Quinta or engaged with other work-related matters, Orla was in Duarte's bed. Or he was in hers. Whichever was closer.

She'd learned that he'd lied about not having tricks. He had plenty, every single one of them astonishing, and in the pursuit of excellence she'd developed a few of her own, one of which she'd tried out in the shower yesterday morning.

In the belief he'd gone off for his habitual early morning swim and she was on her own, she'd switched on the water, lathered herself up and started singing. Terribly. Which was why she generally didn't do it, whatever the genre. But on that occasion, she'd had a song in her head about happiness and rooms without roofs that was driving her nuts and she'd thought, what the hell?

She'd had the fright of her life when a few minutes later Duarte had appeared and asked who was strangling the cat. To cover her mortification, she'd dragged him into the shower with her and then done her very best to wipe the moment from his head, which had only reinforced her newfound belief that the outcome of taking a risk could sometimes be spectacular.

If he had concerns about the beast he'd released, he didn't show it. On the contrary, he was with her every step of the way, as insatiable as she was, as if he, too, were making up for lost time. And maybe he was. Whenever he appeared in the press these days he was conspicuously on his own. If he had had a liaison of any kind, he'd been exceptionally discreet. If he hadn't, if she was the first person he'd slept with since his wife, well, that didn't mean a thing.

'Come for a swim with me,' Duarte said, jolting her out of her thoughts by tossing the sheet aside, getting out of bed and distracting her with the view.

A swim? Orla shivered and her pulse skipped a beat. He'd never invited her along before and she was more than all right with that. So why the change of plan?

'I should get to work,' she murmured with real regret because, although it wasn't going to happen, she'd like nothing more than to mess about in the water with him.

'It's still early.'

'I don't have a costume.'

'No need,' he said, a wicked smile curving his mouth as he threw her a towel. 'There's no one else here.'

She caught it and set it to one side. 'Another time, maybe.'

'I'll make it worth your while.'

She frowned. 'Why the insistence?'

'Why the evasion?'

'All right,' she said with an exasperated sigh since he clearly wasn't going to let this drop and the sight of him all naked and perfect was robbing her of her wits anyway. 'I can't swim.'

His dark eyebrows lifted. 'Really?'

'I was never taught. I can't ride a bike either. Overlooked as a child, remember?'

'You could have learned later.'

'Well, yes, I suppose I could have,' she said, instinctively bristling at the faint but definitely implied criticism, 'but by that point it had become another thing to not be able to do and another thing to avoid. I know it's pathetic. I don't need you to judge.'

'It's not pathetic and I'm not judging. I'm just surprised.'

'It's not *that* uncommon.'

'I will teach you.'

No, he wouldn't, was her immediate response to that. There was no way she was getting in a pool and making a complete and utter fool of herself. Especially not naked. And especially not in front of someone like him, who seemed to be brilliant at everything he did. Besides, she'd become so adept at avoiding anything that involved a beach or a pool she barely even thought about her inability to swim any more.

But now she *was*, she found herself wondering, bizarrely, whether it wouldn't be quite nice to be able to go on holiday somewhere hot at some point. Not that she had the time to go on holiday, or, in fact, anyone to go on holiday with, but two weeks in the sun with no way of cooling off had always been her idea of hell. Come to think of it, three weeks out here, working in the relentless heat and constantly covered in a thin film of sweat hadn't been much fun either from that point of view, and if she was being brutally honest she'd longingly eyed up the pools both here and at the Quinta on more than one occasion.

So maybe she ought to accept a lesson or two. Duarte had taught her about wine. He'd taught her about sex. If she was willing to risk it, he could teach her how to swim, she had no doubt. She trusted him, she realised with a warm sort of glow, and interesting things did tend to happen when he took it upon himself to improve her education. So might this not be a golden opportunity to knock another thing off her activities-to-avoid list?

'All right,' she said, gathering up her courage and assuring herself that, quite frankly, nothing could be more embarrassing than being caught singing in the shower. 'Let's go.'


'Are your hands supposed to be where they are?'

At Orla's side in the pool, Duarte watched her paddle her arms and kick her legs and grinned. 'Absolutely.'

'Only I'd have thought one on the stomach and one on the back would make more sense than one on my bottom and the other on my breast. I feel you might be taking advantage.'

There was no might about it. He took advantage of her every time he got the chance, and where his hands were was no accident. He couldn't stop wanting to touch her. Her skin was as soft as silk and her body was warm and lush. Fortunately for the relentless and mind-boggling need he had for her, she was equally as disinclined to pass up such an opportunity. As he'd suspected, beneath the slightly uptight surface bubbled a volcano that erupted with only the tiniest provocation, and he was more than happy to supply that.

The idea of an affair with Orla really had been one of his best and teaching her to swim hadn't been such a bad one either, he thought, removing his hands from her body with some reluctance and letting her go. Not only did it provide ample opportunity for close proximity and direct contact, but it had also occurred to him that by avoiding anything she wasn't good at and deliberately not trying new things, she must have missed out on a lot. For some reason, he hadn't liked the thought of that and it gave him immense satisfaction to be able to do something about it, although for the life of him he couldn't work out why. But then, he didn't know why he'd invited her for a swim in the first place either when generally he used the time to clear his head and restore the order that she so easily destroyed.

'There,' he said, shaking off the profound sense of unease that came with confusion and focusing instead on her progress across the width of the pool. 'You see? You're swimming.'

'Am I?'

At the edge, she stopped and blinked as she looked back, as if only just realising what she'd achieved. 'Oh, my God, I *am*. You're good.'

'It's not me,' he said, feeling something uniden-tifiable strike him square in the chest and frowning slightly. 'You're the one who had the courage to try and then gave it one hundred per cent.'

The beam she gave him was more blinding than the hot morning sun that was rising above the hills. 'I did, didn't I? How can I ever thank you?'

'There's no need to thank me,' he said as the bril-liance of her smile sizzled through him and ignited the ever-present desire, which was something he *did* understand, at least. 'But if you really insist, I can think of something.'

Orla spent the next week overseeing operations that were going so smoothly they didn't require much at-tention, which was fortunate because her thoughts were becoming increasingly filled with Duarte. She couldn't get enough of him or the conversations they had. They'd talked about work and travel, family and upbringings—everything, in fact, apart from past relationships, as if by unspoken but mutual consent that subject was off the table.

Yesterday, she'd expressed an interest in the wine-making process and he'd taken her on a tour of the vineyard. This morning she'd swum ten full lengths of the pool: three breaststroke, three backstroke, four crawl. Now she was floating about the place, feeling really rather pleased with herself about everything and unable to keep the smile off her face, until reality intruded in the shape of an email from a flower arranger that immediately zapped it.

The ultra-demanding client for whom she'd arranged the iceberg marriage proposal was celebrating it tomorrow with a huge party in a marquee in the grounds of her parents' stately home. Requirements had been extremely detailed and uncompromisingly inflexible, so the news that the ornamental cabbages due to take a starring role in the thirty floral displays had not turned up was not ideal, to say the least.

Half an hour later, however, contrary to Orla's hopes and expectations of an easy fix, 'not ideal' had become 'catastrophic'. Pacing the kitchen, she'd contacted everyone she knew, calling in favours and making promises in return. She'd tried to beg, borrow or steal, but all to no avail, and, as she hung up on the last of her options, panic was beginning to bubble up inside her and a cold sweat coated her skin.

This was her fault, she thought, swallowing down the nausea. She'd become so preoccupied with Duarte and the incredible way he made her feel that she'd taken her eye off the ball. She should have put in a call to all the contractors involved in tomorrow night's event and confirmed the arrangements. She shouldn't have assumed that just because everything was going smoothly here, she could rest on her laurels elsewhere.

So what was she going to do? she wondered, anxiety spreading through her veins and burrowing deep. How was she going to fix this? She didn't have a clue.

She couldn't think straight. Her head was nothing but white noise. She was useless, a complete waste of space. What on earth had made her think she deserved any kind of success? Her pulse was thundering and her chest was tightening. She couldn't breathe. *She couldn't breathe.*

'Orla? Are you all right?'

Duarte's voice filtered through the thick, swirling fog and she was dimly aware of him stalking towards her, vaguely wondering what he was doing there when he'd told her he'd be working at the house today, but mainly thinking, no. She wasn't all right. She wasn't all right at all. The room was spinning and she was hot and dizzy and quite possibly about to pass out.

But she didn't. Seconds before she toppled like a ninepin, a pair of large hands landed on her upper arms, keeping her vertical and holding her steady.

'Look at me.'

Like that was going to help. Looking at him would just make her dizzier. It always did. But sitting was good, she thought woozily as he pushed her down into a chair. Sitting would definitely stop her crumpling into a heap on the floor.

'Breathe.'

'I can't,' she croaked. Her throat was too tight and, because he'd dropped to his knees in front of her and was leaning in close, he was stealing all the air.

'Breathe with me.'

He placed her clammy hand in the centre of his

chest and held it there, covering it with his warm, dry one, and she didn't even have to think about focusing on the rise and fall she could feel beneath her palm. All her senses narrowed in on that one thing, the warm solidity of his body acting like a sort of anchor, calming the chaos whirling around inside her as she instinctively followed his lead until eventually her heart rate slowed and the panic subsided.

'Thank you,' she murmured shakily, faintly mortified and not quite able to look him in the eye as she reluctantly took her hand back.

'What happened?'

'I had a panic attack.'

'Why?'

'There's a national shortage of ornamental cabbages.'

'What on earth are ornamental cabbages?'

'Bedding plants,' she said, lifting her eyes to his and seeing the fierce concern in his expression turn to puzzlement. 'For an engagement party tomorrow night. The iceberg proposal. But there aren't any. Anywhere.'

Duarte sat back on his heels and rested his forearms on his knees, his frown deepening, as if he couldn't see the problem. 'So use something else.'

If only it was that simple. 'Nothing else will do,' she said. 'The bride-to-be was very specific. It's a disaster. A complete and utter disaster.'

At the thought of it, tendrils of renewed panic

began to unfurl inside her and her breath caught, making the dizziness return.

'It doesn't have to be,' he said with enviable calm. 'If you can persuade Isabelle Baudelaire to part with a two-hundred-and-fifty-thousand-dollar bottle of wine, you can persuade this bride-to-be to accept an alternative to ornamental cabbages.'

She stared at him, holding his gaze and taking strength from his steadiness until her head cleared and she could breathe once again. Well, when he put it like that, she probably could. Cardoons had been suggested by one of her contacts. They were as bold as ornamental cabbages, if not bolder, stunning in their own way, and supply wasn't an issue. 'Cardoons might work.'

'And no one will ever know.'

But that wasn't really the point. '*I* will,' she said, swallowing hard. 'I'll always know I screwed up.'

'*You* didn't,' he countered. 'This is not your fault.'

Debatable, but irrelevant. 'I'm still responsible. The buck stops with me.'

'It's a hiccup. Which you will fix. And everything will be fine.'

'It won't be fine,' she said. 'It won't be what the client wanted. It won't be perfect.'

'It will be almost perfect.'

She shook her head in denial. 'Almost perfect is not good enough.'

'It's more than enough.'

It wasn't. It never had been. Second-best wasn't

in her mindset. 'That'll do' was not a phrase she'd ever used. She could understand why he didn't get it. No one ever did.

'You are exceptional at what you do, Orla,' Duarte continued in the same steady vein while she continued to resist. 'I've seen you at work here and watched how you've managed people and handled problems. Focus on the many things you've achieved and trust yourself.'

That was easy for him to say, and it gave her a kick to know that he thought her work exceptional, but she doubted his entire life imploded when he made a mistake. She'd bet he didn't live with a super-critical inner voice that constantly drove him to achieve more and be better. That battered him with insinuations of worthlessness when he was down and made him feel he *deserved* to be overlooked.

He was impossible to overlook. He just had to walk into a room and all heads swivelled in his direction. He came across as supremely confident in who he was and what he did. He was out to prove nothing.

Whereas she was out to prove...

Well, she wasn't quite sure what she was out to prove. Which was odd when she'd always known exactly what drove her. But right now, suddenly, she wasn't sure of anything. Because to her shock and confusion, as everything he'd said spun around her brain like a demented, out-of-control top, she was wondering whether she oughtn't ease up on herself a little. As he'd once pointed out, she did put an immense amount of pressure on herself. She always set herself goals that were slightly out of reach, forever needing more to silence the judgemental devil that lived in her head.

Announcing she'd acquire for Duarte the bottle of Chateau Lafite 1869 was a case in point. It had been a nigh on impossible task. She hadn't slept. She'd been too wired, too focused on the goal. She'd felt no great sense of triumph at having achieved the inconceivable in itself, only at what it had meant for her job and her emotional well-being.

She'd lived like this for the best part of twenty years. She'd never considered perfectionism a flaw— despite what that therapist she'd seen once had insinuated—but maybe he'd been right after all and it was. She knew from experience that it wasn't an irritating little personality quirk. At times it could be hellish. But maybe true perfection was impossible anyway, and if it was, then the pursuit of it was not only wildly unrealistic but also incredibly unhealthy.

How much longer could she go on like this? she wondered, her stomach and her thoughts spinning. She had no time for friends or hobbies. Her to-do lists were out of control. She was heading for burnout. Her doctor would certainly be pleased if she took her foot off the pedal. Her cortisol levels were stratospheric.

And mightn't it be nice to live in the moment for a change instead of either analysing her performance on tasks gone by or thinking about everything she had to do next? Happiness and contentment weren't things she'd ever really thought about, but could she honestly say she was happy? No. She couldn't. Not in the way her siblings were. They were far more sorted than she was. They took setbacks in their stride. They didn't wallow in recrimination and self-doubt when things went wrong. *And* they had the whole relationship thing nailed. Her sister was married and her brother had a long-term girlfriend. She, on the other hand, had been planning to marry a man with whom she had less-than-mediocre sex simply because she refused to admit defeat. She hadn't been jealous of them for years. She found she was now.

So could she unravel two decades' worth of perfectionist traits and allow that good enough *was* good enough? The thought of it made her feel even more nauseous than before, and every cell of her body was quivering with resistance, but something had to change. She couldn't carry on like this. So perhaps she could try it and see how it went, however terrifying.

'You're right,' she said, taking a deep breath and bracing herself for a giant leap into the unknown. 'Cardoons will have to do.'

Noting that the colour had returned to Orla's cheeks and the strength to her voice, Duarte got to his feet and took a surprisingly unsteady step back before turning on his heel, shoving his hands in his pockets and stalking out. He needed air, the more of it he could get and the fresher it was, the better.

Thank God he'd been around to stop her falling, he thought grimly as he emerged into the bright afternoon sunshine and inhaled raggedly, his pulse still hammering at the memory of the sight of her standing there about to swoon. Why he'd changed his mind and opted to work from here instead of staying at the house he hadn't a clue. It wasn't as if he couldn't stay away from her. He wasn't *that* desperate. He was totally in control of the effect she had on him. He didn't *need* to know where she was or what she was doing. He'd decided to head to the kitchen because he was thirsty and felt like an ice-cold beer, not because he'd caught sight of her through the window pacing up and down the flagstones with such a wretched expression on her face that his heart had almost stopped.

But none of that mattered. All that *did* matter was that he'd been in the right place at the right time and a good thing too because if she'd cracked her head on the stone floor she could have hurt herself badly. She could have lain there in pain—or worse—for hours.

Orla evidently wasn't as indestructible as she liked to make out. She had insecurities and vulnerabilities and that meant that he was keeping an eye on her. He wasn't ignoring another woman's emotional well-being. He'd learned that lesson. So from now on, he was sticking to her like glue.

# CHAPTER NINE

ORLA SAT ON the terrace at the Casa, nursing a cup of steaming coffee in the early morning sunshine and contemplating the idea that Duarte was about as ideal a man as it was possible to get. He inspired trust. He could read her body as if he'd studied her for an exam and her mind as if he could see into it. And he was good company.

When she thought about how patient he'd been while she'd freaked out about ornamental cabbages, she melted. He hadn't scoffed about the triviality of bedding plants. He hadn't diminished what to her were very real, very significant concerns. He'd handled her with care and perception and talked her off the ledge, and every time the memory of it slid into her head, she found herself grinning like a fool.

And he might have had a point about the whole 'good enough' thing, she'd grudgingly come to admit. Her demanding bride-to-be had raved about the cardoons, deeming them infinitely superior to the apparently rather lacklustre ornamental cabbage. A minor problem with the drains here had been swiftly, if imperfectly and only temporarily, resolved—which was…well, not too bad, actually. She'd spent years believing that her sense of self-worth was tied up in excelling at everything, but perhaps it didn't have to be that way. Perhaps she could find it in something else. Or even, maybe, someone else…

But Duarte was wrong about one thing. The chemistry that sizzled between them was far from fading. It burned like a living flame inside her, growing stronger every day. Colours were brighter. Smells were more intense. She knew when he was around even if she couldn't see him. Her skin would break out in goosebumps and then, a moment or two later, there he'd be.

In fact, all her senses appeared to be heightened and she felt on top of the world. Her swimming was improving in leaps and bounds. Work was going brilliantly. Progress at the Quinta was steaming ahead and she'd just signed up another ultra-high net worth client, who, happily for her company's bottom line, showed every indication of being all for opulence and extravagance.

Everything was perfect.

Her skin prickled and she couldn't help grinning when a moment later she felt Duarte sweep her hair to one side and drop a hot kiss at the base of her neck.

'I need to go to Porto this evening,' he murmured against her skin, making her shiver and wonder whether there was time for a quickie. 'I have a meeting first thing tomorrow.'

Well, maybe not quite that perfect, she amended, her spirits taking a sudden dip as the blood in her veins chilled. He'd been extremely attentive lately, ever since the ornamental cabbage incident, in fact, and she'd got used to having him around. She didn't like the idea of eating supper on her own. But it would be fine. It wasn't as if she'd miss him or anything. She'd only known him a couple of weeks, and she was hardly addicted to the sex. Honestly. She'd spent innumerable evenings alone. She'd occupy herself with work, just as she usually did.

'OK,' she said, feigning nonchalance with a casual shrug. 'No problem.'

He moved round her and dropped into the seat opposite. 'Come with me.'

At that, those spirits of hers bounced right back and her heart gave a little skip.

Well.

She *could* decline, she told herself, battling the rising urge to grin like an idiot. To prove to herself that she could take or leave him, that she *wasn't* addicted, perhaps. But God, she didn't want to. She wanted to spend the night with him in Porto. She wanted to see where he lived and what he did outside this lovely bubble they currently existed in. The world wouldn't collapse if a problem arose and she wasn't there. She had her phone and she'd keep it on.

So the hyper-critical voice in her head warning

her she was straying into dangerous territory could pipe down. This *wasn't* one of those risks she'd contemplated while paddling at the edge of the river. She was still leaving once the conference was over. She wasn't going to develop any unwise ideas about what this affair of theirs either was or wasn't. But nor was she going to waste a single minute of it.

'I'd love to.'

That evening, Duarte flew her to Porto by helicopter, a forty-five-minute journey that was, in equal parts, terrifying and thrilling.

Terrifying because, despite having organised more such trips than she could count, she'd never actually taken one herself and it was alarming to be hurtling through the air in what amounted to little more than a tin can. And thrilling, because she recalled his asking her to research helicopter options and arrange the lease shortly after he'd signed up to her company's services but never in a million years had she imagined she'd one day occupy the passenger seat.

From the airport they travelled straight to his apartment on the coast, which could not be more different to the properties on the wine estate. It stretched across the entire top floor of a fifteen-storey modern block of what she supposed was cutting-edge design. Light flooded in through acres of glass and bounced off the many reflective surfaces. Rich, gleaming wood and cream marble abounded, and the views of the sea from virtually every angle were stunning. While Orla was a fan of a perfectly positioned cushion or six and the occasional colour-coded bookcase, she could see how this décor would suit Duarte. It was warm, unfussy and unashamedly masculine.

'Nice place,' she said as she walked out onto the vast, lushly planted terrace and joined him at the balcony.

'Thank you.'

He handed her a glass of *vinho verde* and the brush of his fingers against hers sent shivers scuttling down her spine in a way that really she ought to be used to by now but which still caught her by surprise.

'Have you lived here long?'

'Two and a half years.'

He must have moved here soon after his wife had died, she mused, taking a sip and feeling the deliciously cool white wine slip down her throat. It was on the tip of her tongue to ask, because increasingly she found herself wondering about the woman he'd married. What had she been like? The press had painted her as great a party animal as he'd been, but she longed to know more. And what of the overdose? Had that been an accident or deliberate?

However, she couldn't ask. The subject was still far too personal for a brief affair, however intense. Besides, it would ruin the mood of a beautiful evening, so she crushed the curiosity, turned away from the pink-and-gold-streaked sky, and instead focused on the table that sat beneath the pergola strung with fairy lights.

'What's all this?'

'Dinner.'

Well, yes, she could see that, but as she moved closer to peruse the dishes set out on the table her heart began to thud so hard she could feel it in her ears. It was more than dinner. A couple of days ago she and Duarte had had a conversation about culinary loves and hates. And here she could see a platter of langoustines and a dish of plump black olives. A bowl of vibrant guacamole, a basket of ridge-cut crisps and, on a wooden board, sliced impossibly thinly, medium rare steak. All her favourite things.

Her mouth went dry and her head spun for a second. She could totally see how he'd bedded so many women back in the day when he'd lived fast and played hard. Being the object of his attention was like standing for too long in the midday sun—dazzling and dizzying.

'God, you're good at this,' she said, wondering if it would be rude to delay dinner by dragging him off to one of the three bedrooms so she could show him her appreciation properly.

He glanced up from the candle he was in the process of lighting and shot her a wicked grin. 'What, specifically, are you referring to?'

'The whole seduction thing.'

He went still and something flickered in the

depths of his eyes, gone before Orla could even begin
to work out what it was.

'Well, as you know, practice makes perfect,' he
drawled with a shrug, but she noticed that his smile
had hardened a fraction and suddenly, inexplicably,
she felt a bit sick.

Could she have offended him? she wondered, the
wine in her stomach turning to vinegar. Impossible.
His past was no great secret. For years his exploits
had been plastered all over the front covers of the
more salacious global press. She was merely stating
a fact. There was no need to feel bad.

'Right,' she said, her throat nevertheless strangely
tight.

'Take a seat.'

'Thank you.'

'What would you like to do tomorrow while I'm
in my meeting?' he asked, his gaze cool, his expression unreadable.

'I'm not sure.'

'Have a think and let me know.'

While Orla slumbered peacefully in his bed, Duarte sat on the balcony in the warm, still dark of the
night, staring out into the distance, feeling anything
but peaceful.

Dinner had turned out to be unexpectedly awkward. Conversation, for once, had flowed like con-
crete. And it was all because of that comment of hers
about his seduction techniques.

It had stung, he thought, vaguely rubbing his chest. He didn't know why. When applied to his exploits prior to his marriage, it was nothing less than the truth. He'd revelled in the chase and honed his skills to razor-sharp perfection. Yet there'd been no calculation in his decision to have delivered to his apartment all Orla's favourite food tonight. No ulterior motive. They had to eat and it had simply seemed the easiest option. Besides, their affair was blazing. Seduction was unnecessary.

Perhaps, with hindsight, inviting her here had been a bad idea. At the time, he hadn't even had to convince himself that he needed to keep her close so he could keep an eye on her. He'd acted purely on instinct. The last two weeks had been a heady rush of lazy conversation and endless pleasure. As he'd confessed by the river, he liked her, even more so now than he had done then. She was clever and perceptive, self-aware and quick to learn. She had a smile that he wanted to bottle so he could take it out whenever he needed a moment of sunshine, and he found her scent on his pillows so soothing that staying at the Casa didn't bother him any more. Thanks to her original mistake it was unrecognisable anyway, and besides, the new memories they were creating there were doing an excellent job of erasing the old.

Missing even a second of that when she'd soon be gone for good had been deeply unappealing, and he hadn't thought twice about issuing that invitation. But he should have, because it had been rash and reckless and smacked of a man with a shaky grip on his control.

What he'd been thinking over the last fortnight he had no idea. He didn't need to know what made her tick. Her innermost thoughts and opinions were of no importance. She didn't need to know anything about the city of his birth or the place where he lived. And God knew why he'd taken her on a tour of the vineyard the day before yesterday. It wasn't as if he'd wanted her to be impressed by the changes and innovations he'd brought to the business, even though she had been.

He'd come to suspect that the stab to the chest he'd felt when she'd swum a width of his pool on her own had been one of pride. The way she'd handled the cabbage crisis had filled him with admiration, and none of that was necessary. It suggested emotional intimacy, and, unlike intimacy of the physical kind, that played no part in anything. He had no business taking it upon himself to make her see what she was missing out on, living her life the way she did. Instead of ordering all her favourite food last night they should have just eaten out. This was sex without strings and that was it.

But as long as he remembered that there was no need for concern, he told himself, ruthlessly silencing the little voice in his head trying to protest that it might have become more than that. Tonight had been a mistake and some of the things he'd said and done over the last couple of weeks had been dangerously unwise, but there was no point in overanalysing anything or attaching to it a greater significance than it warranted. What was done was done and regrets were pointless. The swimming lessons and conversation could stop easily enough. It was just a question of control.

Tomorrow he'd be in a meeting most of the morning, and when he was done he'd take Orla back to the Quinta. Once there, he'd spend the days they had left proving to her and himself exactly what this fling of theirs was. He'd keep his distance by day and make up for it by night, until she was gone, and everything would be fine.

The following morning Orla was taken on a private tour of Duarte's port house, where she discovered a taste for dry white port and a fascination for the history of his family.

The original founder, Duarte's ancestor, might have come from a humble background, but flushed with vinicultural success, he'd married into the local aristocracy, and ever since then the family's wealth and connections had multiplied. Offspring attended the world's finest schools and best universities, before generally taking up a position in the business.

Judging by the oil paintings that hung on the walls of a gallery built specifically for that purpose, Duarte's looks had been passed down the generations along with his staggering personal wealth. And he'd definitely ended up with the best of them, she'd thought dreamily as she'd stood and stared at his portrait for so long someone had asked her if she'd wanted a seat.

In comparison, she felt rather inadequate and in-significant, so to counter that she visited the most beautiful book shop she'd ever seen, followed by a *pasteleria* famed for its custard tarts, and the exqui-site perfection she'd found in each had made her feel a whole lot better.

At first, Orla had been relieved to be on her own. That awkward moment before dinner last night had been followed by some horribly stilted conversation and then some mind-blowing yet strangely soulless sex. This morning, just before Duarte had left for his meeting, she'd tried to apologise, although she wasn't quite sure what she was apologising for, but he'd looked at her as if he hadn't a clue what she was referring to before kissing her senseless and telling her his car was at her disposal. It was all baffling, not least the switch from soulless to smouldering, and because she felt as though she was suddenly on shaky ground she'd welcomed the breathing space his meeting gave her.

But by the time she arrived back at the airport, she was unexpectedly sorry he hadn't been there to share the experiences with her. At the port house, she'd kept turning to ask him something about one ancestor of his or another, but of course he wasn't there. In the Livraria Lello she'd come across a book about the history of seventeenth-century winemaking in south-west Spain and had wanted to know if he already had it and, if not, whether he might like it. She'd missed him, which was ridiculous when they'd only been apart for a handful of hours and the morning had started off rather oddly, but it was what it was.

She was also filled to the brim with a warm sort of glow that she just couldn't seem to contain. For the best part of a decade she'd organised the lives of other people and, while she loved her job, when it came to things like marriage proposals on icebergs, she couldn't help but feel the occasional pang of envy. This was the first time ever that someone had arranged something solely for her. From the moment they'd taken off yesterday evening she'd barely had to lift a finger. She'd been sublimely fed, luxuriously chauffeured around and, despite the odd uncomfortable moment, been taken care of most excellently. Duarte had made all that happen—for her—and as a result she felt ever so slightly giddy.

'How was your meeting?' she asked when he joined her in the private lounge at the airport, her heart banging against her ribs at the sight of him because the man in a beautifully cut charcoal-grey suit really was something else.

'Productive,' he said, shrugging off his jacket and rolling up his shirtsleeves with an efficiency that left her weak-kneed and breathless. 'I signed a new contract to supply the biggest department store chain in the States.'

'We should celebrate.'

His ebony gaze collided with hers, glittering with a sudden heat that stole the breath from her lungs, and everything fell away, the noise, the lights, the people, everything. 'Hold that thought.'

She held that thought all the way back to the Quinta. She couldn't have shaken it even if she'd wanted to. Forget the landscape. She'd admired it on the journey out. All she could admire now were his hands. His forearms. His profile, complete with the sexiest pair of sunglasses she'd ever seen on a man.

When not occupied with flying the helicopter, his hand was on her thigh, skin on skin, just high enough for her to wish it was higher, covering her where she needed him. She felt increasingly feverish, hot and trembling as if she were on fire. Her stomach was fluttering and her head was buzzing. The pressure in her chest matched in intensity the throbbing between her legs. She was burning up with wanting him and her heart felt too big for her chest. If she didn't have him inside her soon she was going to explode.

The minute they'd touched down on the estate and Duarte had switched off the engine, Orla un-clipped her seatbelt, her hands shaking. He took off his headset and unbuckled himself, but before he could jump out she launched herself across the gap and planted herself on his lap. She smothered his gasp of shock with her mouth and started kissing him with all the wild, unidentifiable tangle of emotions swirling about inside her, until he put his hands on her head and drew her back, his eyes blazing.

'Stop.'

'No,' she breathed raggedly. She didn't want to stop, ever.

'We can't do this.'

What? 'We can.'

'You'll snap the lever.'

'Who cares?'

'I do,' he growled, nudging her off. 'It's my helicopter and I need it functional. Get in the back.'

Orla didn't have to be told twice. With less dignity than she'd have ideally liked, she scrambled between the seats and into the small utilitarian space designed not for passengers but luggage. She landed on the rubberised floor, and a second later Duarte was on top of her, pressing her down with his warm, hard weight and kissing her with a fierce, desperate need that matched her own.

She didn't want finesse. She had no idea what he was muttering in her ear, her Portuguese just not up to that, but she caught the urgency in his voice and guessed that he had no time for it either. While she yanked his shirt from the waistband of his trousers, he shoved her skirt up, dispensed with her knickers and grabbed her knees. He clamped his hands on her hips and shifted, and then his head was between her legs, his mouth on her, hot and skilled.

At the electrifying sensations that lanced through her like lightning, a groan tore from her throat and her chest heaved. Her hands found their way to his head, and her back arched and then, suddenly, she was crying out as spasms of white-hot pleasure racked her body.

She was only dimly aware of Duarte moving to rummage around in his overnight case. She was limp. Blitzed. She'd never shattered so fast and hard that she'd very nearly passed out. Yet, unbelievably, when he lifted her hips and slid into her with one powerful thrust, it triggered a fresh wave of ecstasy that detonated the aftershocks and had her shuddering and shaking all over again.

She wrapped her arms around his neck and her legs around his waist, her heart filled to bursting, and when he hurled them both over the edge into a bright, dazzling shower of stars she wondered how, when the conference was over, she was ever going to let him go.

That was more like it, thought Duarte, rearranging his clothes while his heart rate slowed and his breathing steadied. Frantic and desperate and unexpectedly intense, but, at the end of the day, just sex.

He helped a flushed and dazed Orla off the helicopter, grabbed his bag, and then, with the intention of implementing his plan to avoid her by day at the forefront of his mind, without looking back, strode away.

'Wait.'

He instinctively stopped and spun round. 'What?'

he snapped, irritated beyond belief that he didn't even seem to be able to resist her voice and determined more than ever to keep his distance the minute he'd dealt with this.

'I bought these for you.'

She held out a bag, and for a moment he just stared at it as though it were about to explode.

'Little custard tarts,' she said with a warm smile. 'Your favourite, you said.'

Yes, well, he'd said too much lately. Given away too much. But that stopped now. *'Obrigado.'*

'You're welcome. And thank you for taking me to Porto and arranging everything. No one's ever done anything like that for me before.'

Her eyes were shining and his stomach clenched with even greater unease. What was going on? Why was she looking at him so...*tenderly*? She'd better not be getting any ideas.

'It was hardly a proposal on an iceberg or dinner in front of the Mona Lisa.'

'Doesn't matter. I don't need grand gestures that are frequently style over substance. I had a really great time.'

'Good,' he said bluntly, mentally adding to his plan the need to figure out how he was going to pulverise any potential yet very much misguided expectations she may have. 'I'm returning to the house. I'll see you tonight.'

# CHAPTER TEN

THREE DAYS LATER, after weeks of azure skies and glorious sunshine, the weather changed. As a result of a front moving in from the west, the pressure plummeted and a thick layer of cloud lay heavily over the estate.

All morning, Orla had felt on edge, her stomach with a strange sense of foreboding that had nothing to do with anything on the professional front.

Everything for the conference, which was now in four days' time, was either ready or about to be. Guests had been assigned rooms and arrival details had been finalised. The wine had been retrieved from the cellars and food and staff were arriving, including Mariana Valdez, who thankfully defied the stereotype of the illustrious yet temperamental uber-chef by being utterly charming.

On a personal level, however, it was an entirely different matter. Ever since they'd arrived back from Porto, Duarte had been distant and brooding and worryingly monosyllabic. Citing work, he'd been around less during the day and she found that, as in Porto, she missed him. He'd continued to rock her world at night, more so than before, in fact, which was definitely *not* a cause for complaint, but, while he was at least physically present then, emotionally, she sensed, he was always miles away.

But at least the reason for that wasn't hard to figure out. Today was the anniversary of his wife's death, and if the weight of that knowledge sat like a lump of lead on her chest she couldn't imagine what he must be going through.

She'd woken early this morning, the date flashing in her head like a beacon, and lain there next to him, listening to the gentle rumble of his breathing, her mind racing and her heart aching. How was he going to handle it? Would he want to be on his own? Would he accept her support? Should she brace herself for rejection? Silence? Should she even mention anything?

They weren't exactly friends, and she supposed a brief affair—however intense—wasn't designed to encourage that kind of intimacy. But at the same time, he'd be hurting. How could he not? He might look like a god but at the end of the day he was only human. The whirlwind fairy-tale romance had ended in tragedy. The love of his life was gone for ever. It had to be agony, and if it was solely up to her she'd be there for him. But what would he want?

In the end she'd decided to play it by ear. Whatever Duarte wanted, whatever he needed to get through the day, whether it be space, silence or sex, she'd provide it. She'd be sympathetic and supportive. She could do that, despite her ex once having told her otherwise as their engagement limped to an end. This wasn't someone who'd lost his job due to a corporate restructure and then endlessly moaned about not being able to find a new one without actually putting in all that much effort to facilitate that. This was a man who'd lost his son and beloved wife within six weeks of each other. While it was possible that perhaps she'd been a little harsh on Matt, Duarte's situation could not be more different.

Yet now, tonight, with the rain hammering down outside and the window of opportunity rapidly closing, Orla couldn't stand it any longer. Of all the scenarios that had played out in her head, the status quo had not been one of them. However, all day Duarte had acted as if nothing was different. He'd woken up and she'd braced herself for whatever might be coming her way, but he'd merely reached for her and rolled her beneath him. Then, after grabbing a coffee and a croissant, he'd opened up his laptop and got to work, just as he had yesterday, the day before and the day before that.

Perhaps denial was his coping mechanism. Perhaps he didn't need comforting or to talk about it. The trouble was, because she was aching for him, she *wanted* to talk about it. She *longed* to comfort him. The urge to bring it up had been clamouring inside her all day, swelling and intensifying to an unbearable degree, and if she didn't ask him about it now, when they were at her hotel and privacy was plentiful, then when?

'So how are you feeling?' she said, pulling the sheet over her naked, still languid body, shifting onto her side and propping herself up on her elbow as Duarte emerged from the shower room in a white towel wrapped round his hips and a cloud of steam.

He headed for the window and closed the shutters, treating her to a lovely view of his bare back in the meantime.

'That's the fifth time you've asked me that this evening,' he said tersely. 'And I'm still fine.'

But was he? Really? How could he be?

'You haven't been fine since we got back from Porto,' she said, forcing herself to focus on the mystery of his attitude lately and not his near nakedness. 'You've been distracted and distant.'

'I've been right here.'

'I mean emotionally.'

'What do emotions have to do with anything?'

Right. Well, for him, nothing, obviously. Unfortunately, she was riddled with the things, and they were demanding attention with increasing insistence, which meant that she couldn't let this go.

'You know, if you wanted to talk to me about anything, anything at all, I'd listen,' she said. 'Like you listened to me when I was going on about plants.'

He turned, his expression puzzled. 'What on Earth would I want to talk to you about?'

For a moment, she couldn't breathe. Her lungs had frozen and her throat had closed up. OK, so that hurt, she thought, forcing out a breath. That stabbed at her heart and then sliced right through the rest of her. But she had to persevere because he was clearly in denial and that couldn't be healthy. 'I understand it might be difficult.'

'What might be?'

'Well, today.'

'Why? What's so special about today?'

Surely it didn't need to be said. Surely he didn't need to be reminded. 'It's the anniversary of your wife's death.'

Duarte went very still. His brows snapped together in the deepest frown she'd ever seen on him and he seemed to pale beneath his tan. Shock jolted through her and her eyes widened. The air thickened, the only sound in the room the sound of rain hitting the window like gunshot.

*Had* he forgotten? No. Impossible. It had only been three years. He wasn't the sort of man to let the anniversary of the death of a much-loved wife slip by unnoticed. He couldn't be. She had to be mistaken. It had to be denial, after all.

But the tiny seed of doubt that had taken root in her head was growing a foot a second, and before she could stop herself she said, 'Did you forget?'

'Apparently I did,' he muttered, his jaw so tight it looked as though it was about to shatter.

She gasped and clapped a hand to her mouth. 'Why? How?'

'What business is it of yours?'

His tone was flat, brutal, and hit her like a blow to the gut, even though she knew that the answer to his question was none, no matter how much she might wish otherwise. They weren't in a relationship. They were just having an affair, and one that would soon be over. She had no right to pry. No right to feel eviscerated by the fact that he didn't want to share anything of meaning with her when she'd shared so much. She had no right to anything, but he was toppling off the pedestal she'd had him on, and suddenly that mattered. She wanted to know why.

'How could you?'

'We can't all be perfect.'

'But she was your soulmate,' she said, too agitated and distressed by the notion that he might not be the man she'd thought he was to heed the warning note in his voice. 'The love of your life. I don't understand.'

'Leave it, Orla.'

'But—'

'I said, leave it.'

Still reeling with the shock that had nearly taken out his knees, Duarte grabbed his T-shirt off the bed and yanked it on as if it might provide some kind of protection against the detonation of his world.

Orla's reminder of the date had landed like a grenade that had then gone off. He couldn't believe he'd forgotten. How the hell had it happened? He had no idea, but it did make sense of a lot of the things that had been baffling the life out of him today. Such as the curious glances she'd been casting his way. The bizarre tiptoeing around him and the constant questions about how he was feeling. The concern in her expression and the sympathy in her eyes, which he hadn't been able to fathom and which had only added to the unease that had been gripping him for the last forty-eight hours.

Around lunchtime he'd wondered if she'd started to regret their affair. If she wanted to put a stop to it for some reason that may or may not have had something to do with his strategy of keeping his distance, and had been trying to figure out a way to let him down gently.

The idea that she regretted anything about what they'd been doing had left a strangely sour taste in his mouth, and he'd recoiled in denial at the thought of their affair ending early. But he needn't have worried about that because he'd been wrong. She'd simply remembered the date, that was all, and why wouldn't she? At the time, her company had sent flowers. She'd handwritten him a personal message of condolence. And being good with dates was part of the job, she'd once told him.

He needed to get out of here, he thought grimly as he discarded the towel and pulled on his shorts and jeans. He'd already revealed too much. When, too stunned to exercise his customary caution, he'd admitted he had indeed forgotten the significance of today's date, Orla had been horrified. She'd looked at him as if he'd told her he drowned kittens for fun. She clearly found him severely lacking and he needed no judgement, from anyone, least of all from her. That was precisely what he'd been trying to avoid by allowing the myth of his marriage to perpetuate and the truth to remain buried.

So he ought to leave, pack up his things at the Casa and fly straight to Porto. Before he said or did something he'd *really* regret. Like telling her the truth. He'd have to be insane to do anything as stupid as that. He'd never uttered a word of it to anyone. If he did, to her, if he gave her even half an inch, she'd take a mile. She'd bulldoze her way through his fractured defences and poke around at the exposed weaknesses they were designed to protect. She'd uncover the man he was behind the facade, and she would find him weak. Shameful. Abhorrent.

And yet he was so sick of the secrets, the lies and the guilt. Not even his parents knew the whole truth of what had gone on during the course of his relationship with Calysta. He carried the burden alone, and because he wasn't as good at shouldering it as he liked to tell himself, it was crippling.

He didn't know how much longer he could hold it together. For weeks now, he'd been fraying at the edges, the gruelling schedule he'd adopted to keep a lid on his emotions and get through the days taking its toll. His mother was worried. He'd become short with his staff. It couldn't continue.

So what if he *did* tell Orla what had really happened? Could he trust her to listen without judgement? The feeling that somehow he'd let her down curdled his stomach. He wanted to set the record straight. He wanted to be able to let go of the guilt.

After she'd spilled the truth about her pregnancy Calysta had regularly tried to get him to talk, to no avail, and he was all too aware that if only he had, if only he'd listened, things could have turned out differently.

Might that be the case here? Could shedding the crushing load somehow be cathartic? And what if Orla *wasn't* sickened by the real him? What if somehow she understood? What if she was able to shed some light on the quagmire of his soul?

'I'm sorry,' she said hoarsely, jolting him out of his thoughts as she slid off the bed, still wrapped in the sheet, and reached for her clothes. 'I should never have brought it up. How you choose to handle this is entirely up to you. I should go.'

'No.'

Her gaze snapped to his, her eyes wide with surprise. 'What?'

'Stay.'

'Why?'

He silenced the voice in his head insisting he had to be insane to be considering doing this. The NDA

Orla had signed still held. He had nothing to lose and possibly everything to gain. It would be fine.

'Because I want to tell you what really happened.'

At that, Orla went still, a shiver of apprehension rippling through her as Duarte stalked into the bathroom to hang up his towel.

She had never seen him look so serious, she thought, her heart thudding heavily as she slipped on her T-shirt and the pair of knickers she'd discarded earlier. So haunted and desolate. So completely the opposite of the former playboy she'd caught the occasional glimpse of over the last couple of weeks. She had the unsettling feeling that whatever he wanted to tell her was momentous. It was going to turn everything she thought she knew about him on its head, and that was happening already. Already his halo was shining a little less brightly than before.

Was she ready for that?

God only knew.

But she had told him she'd listen, and this *was* what she'd wanted. To discover the real man behind the image, whoever that might be. The curiosity about his wife and the marriage they'd had, not to mention the shameful jealousy she'd failed to overcome, had become unbearable. And who knew, if he wasn't dealing with everything as stoically as the world believed, maybe she could try to help him in the way he'd helped her to make a start at overcoming her issues? All she had to do was keep calm.in the face of any seismic revelation, which would be a challenge when she was gripped with trepidation, but she'd just have to handle it.

'All right,' she said, settling back against the pillows as Duarte sat down in the armchair that stood in the shadows in a corner of the softly lit room. 'I'm listening.'

He rubbed his hands over his face and then shoved them through his hair. 'Calysta was far from my soulmate,' he said grimly. 'And I didn't love her. In fact, I loathed her.'

Right. Orla swallowed hard, trying to absorb the shock of that when every cell of her body wanted to resist what she was hearing.

'But what about the fairy tale?' she asked, thinking of the pictures she'd seen spread across the pages of *Hello* that March. The bride, beaming, beautiful in white. Duarte looking darkly—although, come to think of it, unsmilingly—handsome in his navy suit as they stood side by side on the battlements of a castle just outside Sintra.

'There was no fairy tale,' he said flatly. 'It ended up being more of a nightmare. We'd been dating for a month when she told me she was pregnant. I married her out of a sense of duty. I felt responsible for her and the baby. That was it.'

No. She didn't want to believe it. She wanted to clap her hands over her ears and screw her eyes tight shut. Yet why would he lie? 'And what about Calysta?' she asked, faintly dreading an answer that would make a mockery of the photos and destroy further an already tarnished image of perfection. 'Did she marry out of duty too?'

He let out a harsh laugh that chilled her to the bone instead. 'Oh, no,' he said, his voice tinged with bitterness. 'She claimed to love me.'

Her throat tightened. 'Claimed?'

A shadow flitted across his face. 'As I said, we'd only known each other a month.'

So what? She'd known him less than that and— Well.

No.

*Her* feelings, whatever they might be, weren't important right now.

'What happened to make you hate her?' she said, determinedly stamping out the emotions hurtling around her system, and focusing.

'We got married when she was twelve weeks into the pregnancy. A couple of months after that we had a discussion about the future. I wanted to focus on building a secure, stable life for our son, she hadn't let up socialising and wanted to carry on. Things got increasingly heated. I told her in no uncertain terms that the partying was to stop and she told me that she'd got pregnant on purpose but really wished she'd chosen someone else.'

And there went another piece of the lovely fantasy, crashing to the ground and shattering. 'What sort of woman *does* that?'

'One who's all alone in the world and desperately

wants a family,' he said. 'Her parents died when she was young. She was very insecure.'

'She was very beautiful.'

'Yes,' he said with a frown. 'She was. I wanted her and I pursued her. But she was clever. She held out.'

'Was she the mistake you referred to when you were telling me about the dangers of letting desire go unaddressed?'

He gave a brief nod. 'It made me want her more. It made me dull-witted and blind.'

'What did you do when you found out?'

He sat back, closed his eyes and pinched the bridge of his nose. 'Lost it,' he said gruffly. 'I realised I'd been trapped. I felt like a fool. I felt somehow betrayed. We had a monumental argument. Two days later I took her to the hospital because she hadn't felt any movement for a while and Arturo had previously been very active. A scan showed that he no longer had a heartbeat.'

That hung between them for a moment during which Orla's eyes began to sting and her heart ached so badly it hurt. 'You don't believe the two events were linked,' she said, barely able to get the words past the lump in her throat.

'Why not?' he said bleakly.

'Is there any evidence for that?'

He shrugged. 'There's no evidence to the contrary. And Calysta certainly blamed me.'

Whatever the truth, the grief and the guilt must have been unbearable. On top of the betrayal he'd already been feeling, he had to have been torn apart. She couldn't *begin* to imagine what it must have been like. 'What happened after that?'

'We buried him and I went back to work, but it was all a blur. We stopped speaking and she was out every night and eventually I told her I wanted a divorce. A week later she took an overdose and died.'

'Deliberately?' she asked, and held her breath.

'I don't know,' he said on a shaky exhale. 'The inquest was inconclusive. All I do know is that I should have noticed what was going on. However I felt about her, she was my responsibility. If I hadn't been so wrapped up in bitterness and resentment, I'd have been able to help. But I was a wreck on all fronts and my judgement was screwed.'

'You were young.'

'I was twenty-seven,' he said with a slow shake of his head. 'Not that young.'

'She can't have been well.'

He regarded her thoughtfully for a moment, his brow creased, then he gave a shrug. 'You're probably right about that. She was very volatile. One minute she was the life and soul of the party, the next she was under the covers with the blinds closed to shut out the light. And she had to deliver Arturo, which must have been hell.'

'She could have been depressed.'

'Or she could have decided that if I was never going to love her then life wasn't worth living.'

Her heart stopped for a second. Did he truly be-

lieve that? If he did, no wonder he was still so affected by what had happened. 'Did she see anyone
afterwards? A doctor? A counsellor?'

'Not to my knowledge.'

'That's a shame.'

'Believe me, I know,' he said bitterly. 'I live with
the guilt of it every single day.'

'I'm not judging.'

His eyebrows lifted. 'Aren't you?'

'No. Of course not.'

'You have impossibly high expectations of people.'

'Well, yes. But—'

His mouth twisted. 'But this is only sex, so you
have no expectations of me at all.'

*What?* Where on earth had *that* come from?

'That wasn't what I was going to say,' she said,
utterly bewildered by his observation, which was so
very wrong. 'I was going to say, I've never been in
a position like that, so how could I possibly judge?
How could anyone? But I do know that what happened wasn't your fault.' Everything else might be up
in the air right now, she knew *that* down to her bones.

'Everything points to the fact that it was,' he said
roughly. 'It *feels* like it was.'

A strangely fierce need to protect surged up inside her. 'No. You're wrong. It was just an impossibly tragic set of circumstances, initiated by a woman
who might have had issues, but was also selfish and
manipulative,' she said, wishing she could rewind

time and rewrite his history. 'I'm not surprised you're angry.'

'I'm not angry. I'm guilty.'

'You are guilty of nothing.'

'I refuse to believe that.'

'You have to.'

'I can't.'

He suddenly looked devastated, as if the weight of the world was crushing him, and the backs of her eyes stung.

'What do your parents say about it all?' she said, swallowing down the boulder in her throat.

'They believe the myth.'

So he'd been handling this all on his own? It made her heart ache for him even more. 'How did that come about?'

'Assumptions were made from the moment Calysta and I got together,' he said. 'In the aftermath they continued, and I was in no fit state to correct them. I was too busy drowning my grief and guilt in wine.'

'Here.'

He nodded. 'The villa where we'd lived on the outskirts of Porto held too many memories. I spent two full months here—you saw the evidence—and then returned to work, coming back only when I needed to escape. There were enough people waiting for me to screw the business up without me giving them more ammunition. It was easier to accept the pity and the sympathy than to explain. I'm not proud of that.'

No, that much was clear. He was tortured by all of it. He blamed himself, and she could see why, but he shouldn't. He'd done what he'd thought was the right thing and been punished for it. He hadn't had the ideal marriage. He'd had a terrible one.

She'd been right to suspect that her view of him would be turned upside down by what he had to say but she hadn't expected the truth to be quite so gritty. Her perceptions of perfection, of him, were shattering all around her. It was huge, overwhelming, and she didn't quite know what to do with it all.

'Do you want to carry on talking about this?' she asked, taking refuge in something that thanks to him she *did* now know how to handle.

His eyes glittered. 'No.'

'Then come back to bed.'

# CHAPTER ELEVEN

CONTRARY TO HIS EXPECTATIONS, Duarte didn't feel better after telling Orla the truth and he didn't feel lighter. After a fitful night, he flew to Lisbon first thing for a meeting with his lawyer about the acquisition of a vineyard in California, an exciting opportunity that would open up new markets and at any other time would have given him immense satisfaction. But there was no sense of triumph. The catharsis he'd hoped for didn't materialise. Instead, all day his stomach churned with a strange sense of dread.

There was no point pretending he didn't know the source of his apprehension. He'd had ample time to figure it out. Instead of returning to the Quinta immediately after the meeting had finished, as had been his original plan, he'd headed to the beach, where he'd spent the afternoon surfing the angry waves of the Atlantic beneath a bruised sky the colour of the Douro's slate-based soil in an effort to unravel the chaos swirling around inside him.

He'd allowed their affair to spiral out of control,

he knew now with unassailable certainty. From the moment he'd threatened Orla with scuppering the agreement she'd made with Isabelle Baudelaire, he'd arrogantly assumed that he was in charge, and that that was where he'd remain. But he'd been wrong. Somehow, without his even being aware of it, the power had been gradually slipping away from him until she held it all, and he hadn't even considered that a possibility. Once again, he'd been so consumed with the present that he'd been blind to the danger of the future.

She'd sneaked through his defences and stolen control of his thoughts. She'd had him changing his plans on a whim and behaving in a way that he simply didn't recognise and certainly couldn't explain. Such as teaching her to swim or encouraging her to believe that life didn't have to be perfect, that it was all right to fail. What business of his was any of that?

Things between them had become too intense. He'd wanted a distraction, sure, but he'd never expected to it to take over so completely. He'd never anticipated the attraction intensifying instead of dissipating. Somewhere along the line their affair had turned into something that was more than just sex, despite his efforts to convince himself otherwise. He'd told her the truth about his marriage because he felt he could trust her with it, which was stupidly rash and beyond dangerous. It was true that they'd been working well together for several years now and she'd signed an NDA, so she couldn't do anything with the information, but that didn't mean it was all right to be sharing with her something so intensely personal, something that no one else knew.

And when had wanting to live up to her expectations become so important? He had no idea about that either. All he knew was that the moment she'd told him to come back to bed last night was the moment he'd realised how petrified he'd been of her judgement. How badly he *hadn't* wanted her to find him shameful and abhorrent. The relief that had flooded through him when it had become clear that she didn't had nearly had him weeping with gratitude.

He'd sworn he would never again allow a woman to hold all the power, he reminded himself grimly as he angled the helicopter and the Quinta came into view far below, and he had no intention of breaking that vow. He would not allow emotion to cloud his judgement and he would not end up in a position where he could be held accountable for someone else's well-being and destroy that someone along the way.

So he had to end things with Orla before he was in so deep that happened and he couldn't get out. She represented too great a threat to the way he wanted to live his life, free from the responsibility and commitment that experience had proven he couldn't handle. It wouldn't be fair to her, either, to let things carry on. He'd caught the way she looked at him sometimes, with stars in her eyes and a dreamy smile on her face. He didn't deserve stars and dreams. He'd never deserve her, so there was no pointing in wanting her any more.

All was set for the conference. There was no need for her to remain in Portugal. He'd told himself to back off once before and been too damn weak to follow it through, but this time it would be different. This time, the minute he landed, he'd track her down. He'd tell her it was over and send her home, whatever it took, and absolutely nothing was going to stop him.

*Finally.*

As the familiar rumble of the Land Rover cut through the still of the night, Orla jumped off the bed and ran to the window. Headlights lit up the road to the hotel but she could just about make out the shape of Duarte in the driving seat, and God, it was good to see him. He'd been gone *such* a long time. Because he'd been due back mid-afternoon and her texts had gone unanswered, she'd been going out of her mind with worry. She'd been on the point of calling the police when she'd received a reply from him asking where she was.

Waiting for him to return had been agonising. She'd done a lot of thinking while he'd been away and come to a number of conclusions that she ached to share with him. Given the lull in activity at the Quinta, the calm before the storm as it were, she'd had to do *something* to fill the time and it was inevitable that her thoughts would be filled with him, with herself, with them.

Especially after last night.

She understood him so much better now, she thought, her heart thundering as he got out of the car and slammed the door behind him. He was racked with guilt that in her opinion was very much misplaced. No wonder he'd flipped out so badly when he'd found her asleep in his bed the day they'd met. She'd invaded his privacy and caught a glimpse into his carefully guarded soul. She'd dug up the truth he'd kept buried and he'd resented that.

Every time she recalled what he'd been through, she wanted to weep. No one deserved to suffer such torment and it broke her heart that he'd had to deal with it alone. Had she been able to help him last night? God, she hoped so, but who knew? He'd been quiet this morning before he'd left for Lisbon.

She'd been so wrong to place him on a pedestal, she'd realised over a cup of tea this afternoon. He'd never claimed to be perfect. That had been all on her. She'd taken the bits of him he'd allowed her to see and judged him accordingly. But she'd been foolish to do so. No one was perfect. And what on earth gave her any right to judge anyone anyway?

Her ex had been right all along. She hadn't been particularly supportive or sympathetic when he'd needed it. The minute he'd told her he'd been axed as part of a strategy to reduce headcount, he'd plummeted in her estimation because she'd thought he clearly hadn't been good enough to be retained. But that had been grossly unfair of her. The loss of his job hadn't been his fault and she should have recognised the massive collapse of confidence he'd suffered because she experienced the same on the rare occasion she failed.

She *did* have expectations of people that were unjustly high, she'd thought, accepting the guilt washing over her that was nothing less than she deserved. She did judge. And because of it, she subconsciously pushed people away. Colleagues, potential friends, the occasional fiancé... She'd always told herself that she didn't have time for relationships of any kind, but in reality she'd always been pretty unforgiving of other people's foibles, and no one needed that kind of pressure. As a result, she was always on her own, which had never bothered her before, but now, she found, did. A lot. She hadn't realised how lonely she'd become until she'd met Duarte and embarked on an affair during which she was with him pretty much all day every day.

Most things in life, she'd discovered in the course of her soul-searching, weren't as black and white as she'd always assumed. They lay somewhere in the grey, the middle ground. And, while this was uncharted territory for her, it was territory that she was determined to explore because she was beginning to think that, contrary to the beliefs she'd held for so long, there was actually little good about perfectionism and having impossibly high expectations. Both made for isolation and loneliness. Both inevitably led to wholly unnecessary disappointment.

If she was being brutally honest, to discover that Duarte had feet of clay, that he was as flawed and fallible as she'd learned she was, was something of a relief. Now that she'd allowed 'good enough' into her way of thinking she'd been worrying about being able to match up to him. But now she felt that perhaps she *could* match up. At least she hoped so. Because she didn't want this to end. She wanted him. For far more than an affair. She wanted him for ever, because she was head over heels in love with him.

From the moment she'd taken his call and signed him up shortly after his marriage three and a half years ago, she'd been fascinated by him. Every time his name had popped up on her phone her heart beat that little bit faster. For every request he'd made she put in that little bit more effort. The reality of the man far outclassed any dream she'd ever had. He was patient. Thoughtful. Not to mention hot as hell and able to make her come in under thirty seconds. And he'd shone a light on some of her deepest, darkest fears and reduced them to the faintest of shadows.

But how did he feel about her?

Their affair wasn't just about sex. It never really had been. Right from the beginning he'd looked out for her. He'd taught her how to swim and shown her another, better, way to live her life. He'd given her belief in herself that didn't come from the pursuit of perfection, and he'd told her the truth about his marriage. All that had to mean something, but what?

Did she dare to find out?

It would be a massive risk, she thought, her heart hammering even harder as she heard footsteps thud along the corridor outside her room. They hadn't known each other long. They both had issues that needed working through. But perhaps it was a risk she ought to take, because they could be so good for one another. And now she knew there was no ghost to compete with, what was stopping them from carrying on and seeing where things went?

At the sharp rap on the door, Orla practically jumped a foot in the air. She spun round from the window and headed to open it, her feet barely touching the floor. Her heart was fit to burst with hope and anticipation, her smile wide and giddy as she flung back the door, but at the sight of the expression on Duarte's handsome face, she froze.

His jaw was tight and his eyes were dark. He looked tense, on edge, and something about the way he was standing sent a bundle of nerves skittering through her. He seemed braced for something, something unpleasant.

A cold sweat broke out all over her skin and her pulse began to race. Had something happened? What? She couldn't tell. His face was completely unreadable.

'Come in,' she said, instinct warning her to proceed with caution as she stood to one side to let him pass.

But he didn't move an inch. 'I won't, thanks.'

What? Why not? 'Bad meeting?'

'The meeting was fine.'

'So what's wrong?' Because something was definitely up. Could it be a delayed reaction to last night's conversation? If it was, whatever he needed from her, she'd give it to him. She'd give him everything. Especially if he actually came into her room.

'Nothing's wrong,' he said, thrusting his hands into the pockets of his trousers. 'How was your day?'

'Professionally uneventful, personally illuminating.'

He frowned at that, just for a moment. 'Everything ready for Friday?'

'Yes.'

'Good. Then your services are no longer required.'

Oh? What did that mean? 'Well, I wouldn't put it quite like that,' she said with the hint of a knowing grin despite the faint ribbon of anxiety beginning to wind through her. 'My...*services*...are available until Sunday.' Hopefully even beyond.

'I'm serious,' he said. 'You should go home. Tomorrow.'

The smile slid from her face. Tomorrow was Wednesday. The conference started on Friday. What was going on? 'I should be here in case things go wrong.'

'They won't.'

'When did you become the expert?'

'I'll call if there's a problem.'

Her pulse sounded in her head. Her mouth dried,

and as the truth dawned, her stomach rolled. 'You're not joking, are you?' she said with difficulty. 'You really want me to go.'

'Do I look like I'm joking?'

No. She'd never seen anyone appear to be joking less. His jaw was so tight it looked as if it were about to crack. He was pale beneath his tan, but there was no mistaking the intent behind his words. He was resolute, impenetrable. He was batting away every point, every protest she made, and would continue to do so.

And then it hit her like a blow to the head that *she* was the unpleasant business. While she'd been carefully picking up the pieces of her shattered foundations and putting them back together in a different, better way so that she could dream of a future with him, he'd been revving up to tell her to leave.

'Why?' she managed, her throat impossibly tight.

'Your work here is done.'

'And what about us?'

'There is no us.'

His face was utterly unreadable and it was horrible. Who *was* this? Where was the man she'd fallen in love with? She didn't recognise the ice-cold stranger before her.

She swallowed hard, feeling nauseous and faint. 'There could be.'

A muscle hammered in his jaw. 'There won't be.'

'Does this have anything to do with last night?'

'No,' he said with the barest of shrugs. 'I've sim-

ply had time to reflect on things and come to the realisation I've had enough.'

While she'd come to the realisation that she hadn't
had nearly enough.

The pain that shot though her at that was swift
and harsh. It pulverised reason and made her desperate. It made her reckless. 'I'm in love with you.'

The only indication he even heard her was a
flicker of something in the depths of his eyes, but it
was gone before she could identify it. 'I regret that
happened.'

Orla stared at him, frozen in shock, the air trapped
in her lungs while the world about her collapsed. And
then, charging through the rubble, came fury. He *regretted that happened*? What the *hell*? How dared
he dismiss her feelings like that, as if nothing they'd
shared mattered, as if *she* didn't matter? How could
he be so brutal? After everything? The hot, wild
tangle of emotions swirling through her coalesced
into one cold, hard lump and settled in her chest, and
then, blessedly, she could feel absolutely nothing.

Up until this very moment, despite how this little
chat had developed, she would have given him the
benefit of the doubt. She'd have slept on it, tracked
him down in the morning and tried to figure out what
was behind all this. But not now. Now he'd drawn an
indelible line in the sand and obliterated both what
they'd had and what they could have had. Which
meant that she wasn't going to hang around when she
was very obviously not needed. So, contrary to his

instructions—instructions! As if *he* had the right to dictate what she was to do when this was her *job*—she wouldn't be here tomorrow. She'd leave tonight. He and his bloody conference didn't deserve even a second's more consideration.

'Well, that seems to say it all, doesn't it?' she said numbly.

He gave a curt nod. 'I believe so.'

'Goodnight, then.'

'Goodnight.'

And with that, he turned round and strode down the corridor, leaving her standing there, stock still, chilled to the bone and wondering what the hell had just happened.

Duarte didn't recall getting to his car and driving back to the Casa. It was only when he switched off the engine and killed the headlights that he realised that his palms were sweating and his entire body was trembling.

With relief.

That was what it had to be, he told himself as he shakily stepped down from the Land Rover and inhaled great gulps of air.

Because he'd done what he'd set out to do and he hadn't faltered. He hadn't been blown away by the dazzling smile she'd greeted him with. He'd ruthlessly ignored the tsunami of pleasure that had rushed through him at the sight of her, and he'd resisted the fierce urge to push her back, slam the door and tumble her to the bed. When she'd told him she was in love with him he'd steeled himself so successfully that the overwhelming desire to sweep her into his arms and never let her go hadn't even made it into his head. He'd remained strong and in control at all times, even in the face of her evident shock and anger once she'd finally got the message.

As a result, he'd avoided a highly dangerous liaison that would have inevitably ended up in pieces. He didn't want to hold Orla's emotions in his hands. He couldn't be responsible for them. He didn't want her love. He wasn't capable of returning it. He'd only destroy it.

But disaster had been averted, he thought grimly as he stalked into the dark, quiet house. Tomorrow she'd leave. He was safe. More importantly, *she* was safe. So it was all good.

Thanks to the savage anger coursing through her veins like fire, Orla held it together as she packed up her things, checked out and then drove the two hundred and fifty kilometres from the hotel to the airport in the early hours of the morning. She spent the entire duration of the first flight back to London grimly thanking her lucky stars that she'd discovered Duarte's true colours before humiliating herself by begging him to let her stay. He wasn't at all the man she'd thought he was and she'd had a narrow escape, she'd told herself over and over again in the taxi from Heathrow to her flat. Such a narrow escape.

It was only when she walked over her threshold and closed the door on the world outside that she fell apart. Exhausted, miserable and wretched, her armour falling away and vanishing into thin air, she dumped her bags in the hall and sank to the floor.

The pain that lanced through her then was unlike any she'd felt before. It sliced open her chest and tore her heart to shreds. It whipped the breath from her lungs and put a sting in her eyes. She thought she'd been devastated when Matt had broken up with her, but that was a scratch compared to this. This was true agony.

How had things gone so badly wrong? she wondered as the sting became tears that seeped out of her eyes and flowed down her cheeks. They'd been going so well. She'd had no sign that anything was amiss. Apart from the strangely charged moment she'd handed him the custard tarts on their return from Porto, perhaps. At the time, she hadn't paid it much attention. She'd been too starry-eyed from the scorching encounter in the helicopter and too overwhelmed with emotion for nuance. But now she thought about it, his jaw had been rigidly tight then too. Perhaps she'd gone too far, overstepped a line.

And she'd done it again by pressing him on his marriage. Deep down he couldn't have wanted to talk about it. It was a harrowing tale. She should never have indulged her curiosity. She should never have forced him to relive it. Yes, she'd tried to backtrack and leave him in peace at the time, but she wouldn't have been able to for long. It would have festered until the belief that she was right would have pushed her to demand the truth anyway.

What had she been thinking? What on earth had made her believe that she could possibly help? She knew nothing of what he'd been through. Nothing. She wasn't right. About anything.

She'd been so stupid to allow herself to fall in love with him, she thought on a heaving, painful sob. She'd been swept away by the romance of the location and the situation and read too much into everything. Despite the intensity of their affair, the conversation and the thoughtfulness, they hadn't had a real relationship. They'd barely stepped off the estate. It had been a one-scene fantasy. The perfect fantasy, in fact, until reality had intruded and smashed it to bits.

She'd been a fool to believe in it and as deluded as Isabelle Baudelaire to assume that she could be the one to bring him back to life and teach him to love. She wasn't that person. She wouldn't ever be that person. It was truly over. There was no coming back from this. So what on earth was she going to do now?

# CHAPTER TWELVE

AT EIGHT O'CLOCK in the morning Duarte addressed the team Orla had been working with and updated them on her departure. The news that she'd left without so much as a goodbye was greeted with looks of surprise and expressions of disappointment. He, however, did not share either sentiment. He'd have only been surprised if she'd defied his order to go, and all he felt was relief.

Everything had turned out exactly as he'd planned and, as he stalked into the bustling kitchen of the Quinta in search of the coffee that he needed to get through the day after a largely sleepless night, he felt as if he could breathe for the first time in weeks. He was free. Of commitment, of responsibility, and, more importantly, of all the emotions he'd felt whenever he'd been with her.

He'd definitely done the right thing in sending her away, he told himself as he retrieved two cups from the cupboard, frowned, and returned one. He'd soon get used to being on his own again. He'd only known her properly for three weeks. By Monday he'd be back in Porto, back to work, and what had happened here would fade until it became nothing more than a distant memory.

Besides, it wasn't as if he couldn't manage this coming weekend. He ran a billion-euro business. He could handle a two-day conference. How hard could it be? He didn't need Orla and her unsettling insights. He wasn't going to miss her in the slightest. He was perfectly all right. Couldn't be better, in fact, and everything was going to be fine.

But it wasn't fine. It wasn't fine at all.

Thanks to Orla's meticulous planning and preparations, the conference itself went off without a hitch. The weather had improved and the Quinta looked spectacular. The food and drink had been exceptional, issues had been discussed and problems had been solved. Any doubts anyone may have had about his ability to run his company had been well and truly squashed.

However, this boat trip up the Douro, to round off the weekend, was proving problematic.

Duarte hadn't given much thought to the route. He'd left the logistics up to the crew. But he should have insisted on knowing the plan, because they were heading for the spot where he'd taken Orla for a picnic and now, no matter how busy he'd been over the last couple of days, no matter how hard he forced himself to focus on the tour and entertain his guests this afternoon, she was all he could think about.

Despite his intentions to the contrary, he had missed her. The Casa was quiet and empty without her vibrant, dazzling presence, yet filled with the memories that they'd created together, which fractured his sleep. To his intense frustration, he'd been seeking her out all weekend. Every time it hit him that she wasn't there, bleak disappointment struck him in the chest, as confusing as it was unwelcome. And increasingly, when he thought of the way he'd sent her home, he didn't feel relief. His stomach invariably knotted and a weight sat on his chest, the regret so intense it made his head spin. His appetite had disappeared and a dull heaviness had seeped into every cell of his body.

Yesterday evening, after his guests had retired for the night and the staff had returned to the village, he'd headed for the vines, hoping that the peace and tranquillity of the hills and the warm scent of the earth would soothe the chaos swirling around inside him as it so often did. But he'd found no solace there. In fact, with no guests to distract him, his unsettled thoughts had turned to Orla even more and she'd become a burr, sticking to his skin, impossible to remove.

Today, the creeping restlessness had expanded and spread, its tendrils reaching into every inch of him, and it was now crushing him on all sides. He stood at the polished wood railing that ran around

the bow of the cruiser, staring at the bend in the river
around which lay the beach, breathing in deep lungs-
fuls of air while inside his guests helped themselves
to a sumptuous buffet. But nothing he did seemed to
relieve the pressure. It was in his head. In his chest.
Everywhere.

His knees shook and he gripped the railing so
tightly his knuckles went white, but it was too much,
and suddenly, unexpectedly, something inside him
snapped. His defences splintered and a wild rush
of emotions, thoughts and realisations rained down
on him.

He missed her, he loved her, and he'd been the
biggest of fools to have taken this long to realise it.
He'd been thinking about her for months, long before
he'd actually met her. Making spurious requests to
fill in the time between the genuine ones, just so he
could hear her voice. That was how he'd ended up
with the helicopter. He could have easily told his sec-
retary to liaise with her. He hadn't had to get personally involved. But their conversations had triggered
fantasies that had become addictive, fantasies that
he knew now had come nowhere close to the reality,
and he hadn't wanted to let that go.

For three years he'd been petrified of a relationship. Of commitment. Of letting anyone get too close
and then destroying them with his staggering self-
absorption and emotional obstinacy. But there was
nothing terrifying about what he'd been doing with
Orla. He *liked* the way he'd behaved with her—be-

fore he'd screwed everything up—*and* the fact that traces of the man he used to be had returned. She was not Calysta and this was not the same.

For days he'd been resisting and denying the points she'd made about his marriage with every bone in his body because he was too afraid of the possibility of a relationship opening up and him wrecking it. But perhaps Orla was right. Perhaps none of what had happened had been his fault. The terrible day of the scan, the obstetrician had talked about a heart defect as the most likely cause of Arturo's death in the womb, but he'd barely listened. He'd just recalled the savage argument two nights earlier, and the link between the events had seemed so damn obvious. He'd held himself to blame ever since, but maybe he had to accept that it had simply been nature at its most cruel.

And as for Calysta, after Arturo's funeral he should have been around more instead of immersing himself in work. However much he'd despised her at that point, however much he'd been grieving for the son he'd badly wanted despite the circumstances of his conception, he should have considered what she'd been going through. But he would never have loved her the way she'd needed him to, whatever the circumstances, and she would never have been able to accept that.

So could he let go of the guilt? He wanted to. God, how he wanted to. Because he wanted Orla back. He wanted her trust and her love. He wanted it all.

But whether she'd even agree to see him was anyone's guess. The look of devastation on her face when he'd told her he was sorry she'd fallen in love with him still haunted his dreams. Out of sheer fear, he'd been cruel and callous. He felt sick and his chest ached to think of it.

Could he fix the godawful mess he'd made of things? He'd do his damnedest to try. As he'd once told Orla, he too had goals, and this was his biggest, most important one ever. So he'd do whatever it took, however long it took, and this time he would not screw it up.

Releasing his white-knuckled grip on the rail, Duarte turned on his heel and stalked into the cockpit to address the captain.

'The trip is over,' he said, his jaw set and his entire body filling with resolve. 'Turn the boat around.'

'Orla!'

Orla had barely stepped out of the lift when Sam Hamilton, her co-CEO for the time being, accosted her in the lobby of their fifth-floor offices in London's West End.

At his expression, the little hairs at the back of her neck shot up and her pulse skipped a beat. The last time he'd looked this serious, three days ago, in fact, he'd told her he planned to retire within the next twelve months, and if she wanted it the business would be hers. The news should have had her punching the air in triumph. Instead, she'd just about managed to muster up a weak smile and mutter a half-hearted 'thank you', but that had been it. Despite the endless talking-tos she'd given herself recently, she was still so damn sad about Duarte.

But enough was enough. A weekend of moping about, immersed in self-pity and misery, was plenty. Any more ice cream and she'd turn into a pistachio. Who needed a relationship anyway? How many of them failed? She didn't know the statistics, but she knew it was a lot, and she wanted none of it.

No. Instead, she'd decided it was time for change. She was going to focus on her issues. She'd figured her insecurities and fears would exist whether she failed or succeeded, so she'd start with them. She'd always associated her sense of self-worth with a need to achieve, but why did it have to be that way? Why couldn't she find it elsewhere? Say, from her job? From friends? From who she was, which wasn't *so* bad really? So she was going to be less unforgiving. Of herself and other people. She'd learn to accept criticism without getting all defensive about it and start to build some proper, healthy relationships.

She'd forget about Duarte and the bittersweet memories soon enough. Just because she thought about him constantly didn't mean that she would for eternity. She'd talk herself out of it eventually. She talked herself out of things all the time. And, quite honestly, so what if she had fallen in love with him? It was nothing to be ashamed of, although it was regrettable that she'd told him. Unfortunately, you couldn't choose whom you loved and you couldn't make them love you in return. You just had to accept things as they were, and try to avoid the chaos, mess and misery that was love for a very long time.

At least the super-loud, super-critical voice in her head had gone. She wasn't perfect, nothing in life was, and that was OK. She *was*, however, utterly drained by all this self-analysis on top of everything that had transpired before and, quite frankly, she could do without the hassle of whatever it was that had Sam in such a state so early. But she was a professional, so she'd take it in her supremely capable stride.

'Sam,' she said, plastering a smile to her face and hoisting her satchel higher onto her shoulder as they set off across the lobby. 'Is there a problem?'

'We've had a complaint.'

Oh? Her heart plummeted. No wonder he was agitated. Complaints were unwelcome, and, thankfully, rare. 'What is it?'

'It's more a case of who.'

Her eyebrows lifted. 'Who?'

'Yes. He's in your office.'

'Who is?'

'Duarte de Castro e Bragança.'

Orla froze mid-step, her head spinning and her heart suddenly pounding. No. That couldn't be the case. What did he have to complain about? Sam had informed her that the conference had been a success from start to finish, although apparently the river cruise had ended rather abruptly and ahead of schedule. And why was he in *her* office anyway?

'Can't you deal with it?' she said, her stomach clenching at the thought of him in her space, breathing her air and looking around her things. 'He's your client now.'

'I believe that's the complaint.'

What? He was the one who'd necessitated the switch with his brutal dismissal of her. So how dared he saunter in here and turn her world on its head again? This was *her* space. Her *sanctuary*.

Well.

Whatever.

Duarte didn't bother her any longer. Did Not Bother Her. She had no need to be distressed by this latest turn of events. She was immune to his charms now. She'd handle him with polite professionalism, get to the bottom of his so-called complaint and then she'd send him on his way.

'Fine,' she said flatly, setting her jaw and straightening her spine. 'Leave it with me.'


At the sound of the door to Orla's office opening, Duarte, who'd been pacing up and down in front of the window, oblivious to the view, oblivious to anything other than the drumming of his pulse and the desperate need to put things right, spun round.

Orla closed the door behind her and then turned to him, and a wave of longing crashed over him. He'd missed her. He'd missed her immeasurably. How on earth could he have sent her away? What had he been thinking?

'Good morning,' she said with a practised smile that didn't reach anywhere near her eyes, and which he hated, but then, he hadn't expected an easy ride. He deserved the ice and the bristling even if it did chill him to the bone and fill him with shame.

'Good morning.'

She strode over to the desk and sat down, so cool, so professional, so hard to read now. 'Have you been offered coffee?'

'I have,' he said, seating himself in a chair on the other side of her desk and linking his hands to stop them shaking.

'Good. So. I understand you have a complaint.'

'I do.'

'What is it?'

'I called to speak to you and was told that you'd given my account to someone else.'

'Yes,' she said with a brisk nod. 'To Sam. My co-CEO.'

He swallowed with difficulty. 'Why?'

'Because he's excellent.'

'That's not what I meant and you know it.'

'We crossed a line, Duarte,' she said bluntly, her voice completely devoid of expression. 'Do you honestly think we could have carried on working together after what happened at the Quinta?'

'Which part in particular are you referring to?'

'All of it.' She swivelled round to switch on her computer. 'It was a mistake from start to finish.'

'You don't make mistakes.'

'I do. And I've discovered recently that that's fine.'

He frowned. They'd been many things, but a mistake was not one of them. Did she really think that? Had he done that to her with his cowardice and fear?

'Was there anything else?'

Oh, yes. He wasn't done. Not by a long shot. He'd prepared a speech. He'd been practising. 'I've barely begun.'

'Well, I have a meeting in,' she glanced at her watch, 'ten minutes. So I can give you five.'

Then he didn't have a second to waste. This was the most important moment of his life. His entire future happiness depended on it. He took a deep breath and focused. 'I wanted to apologise for our last conversation,' he said gruffly, regret pouring through him at the memory of it. 'For the way I behaved. It was appalling and unnecessary, and when I think of it I am deeply ashamed.'

'Accepted,' she said with a dismissive wave of her hand.

'I wanted to explain.'

'No explanation necessary.'

His heart began to pound. 'You were right about everything.'

'Not any more, I'm not. I'm through with all that.'

What did that mean? Was she through with him

too? A bolt of pure panic shot through him. 'I'm in love with you.'

She stared at her monitor, utterly still for a moment, and then she clicked her mouse and adjusted her keyboard. 'That's…regrettable,' she said, and typed in what could have been her password.

Not that he was capable of that level of logic. He was reeling with the shattering realisation that he'd blown it. For good. The flatness of her tone… The way she couldn't look at him… Her choice of words, which was no coincidence… One mad, terrible conversation that had been driven by the demons that he'd foolishly allowed to override everything else and he'd ruined the best thing that had ever happened to him.

Suddenly Duarte couldn't breathe. The shock of what he'd done and the realisation that it was undoable had winded him. His vision blurred. His chest was tight. He couldn't speak for the pain scything through him.

'You'll be in good hands with Sam' came her voice through the fog. 'And now, if you'll excuse me, I really am very busy.'

Yes, he could see that. Whatever it was that she was looking at was demanding her full attention. She was scrolling and typing, scrolling and typing, while his world was splintering into a million tiny pieces.

'Right,' he said gruffly, his throat sore, his entire body trembling. 'I see. In that case, I won't waste another second of your time.'

He got up in a daze. Turned to leave, grateful for the fact that his legs would get him out of here. But then at the door, his hand on the handle, he stopped. No, dammit. That *wasn't* it. He wasn't having this. He'd come here for a reason. He had things to say and they needed saying. He'd vowed on the boat to do whatever it took and that was precisely what he *would* do.

Squaring his shoulders and taking strength from the determination and adrenalin rocketing around his system, Duarte spun back, and froze at the raw, naked misery that crumpled Orla's face for a split second before it disappeared and her expression was once again unreadable.

But he'd caught a glimpse behind the mask, thank *God*, and, while it killed him to see, it also had hope and relief roaring through him because she wasn't as indifferent to him as she was trying to make out. She wasn't indifferent at all.

Why, oh, why couldn't Duarte have left? Orla thought desperately, her heart racing as he slowly stalked back towards her. She'd been doing so well, holding the emotions raging through her at bay and clinging on to her dignity even though it had taken every drop of strength she possessed. So well to steel herself against his declaration of love, which meant nothing when the memory of Tuesday night was still so raw.

Why had he had to turn around at that precise moment when the pain of what she'd lost had become too much? There was no chance he hadn't caught the brief slip of her deliberately icy facade. Gone were the nerves she thought she'd detected in him a moment ago. He was all steely purpose, his jaw set and his eyes glinting darkly as he bypassed the chair he'd earlier vacated and came to perch on her desk, so close she could reach out and touch him if she wanted to.

'I still have four minutes,' he said, gripping the edge tightly as he gazed down at her.

Orla pushed her chair back, out of his mind-scrambling orbit, and sat on her hands. 'Three and a half actually.'

And that was three and a half too many. How long would her strength hold out? Already, his proximity was battering away at her defences. Already she could feel herself weakening.

'I'm so, so sorry,' he said gruffly. 'For everything that I said on Tuesday night. I was terrified of my feelings for you. I wasn't ready to let go of the past. Ever since Calysta died I've been wrapped up in the idea that because what happened to her was my fault, I can't be responsible for someone else's emotions. But you were right. About so much. Especially the guilt and the blame. And if I've been wrong about that, then I'm wrong about the rest of it. I love you, Orla. I think I've been falling in love with you ever since I asked you to research helicopters for me when I didn't even need one.'

Her heart thundered in her ears, and, with her armour suffering blow after blow, she simply couldn't keep the icy front up any longer. 'I offered you everything,' she said hoarsely as all the hurt and pain broke through to batter her from every angle.

'I know.'

'You were cruel.'

His expression twisted and the sigh he gave was tortured. 'I know.'

'You hurt me.'

'Irrevocably?'

'I don't know.'

He stared at her, regret and sorrow filling his gaze, and then he swallowed hard and gave a nod. 'I understand,' he said roughly. 'Right. Well. That was all I wanted to say. I should go.'

He pushed himself off the desk and, in a split second that seemed to last a year, Orla's brain spun. Was she really going to let him leave? After everything he'd told her? When it had to have cost him so much to say? Despite everything she still loved him madly and she wanted nothing more than to throw herself into his arms and never let go.

But was she brave enough to do it? Just because he'd recognised his hang-ups didn't mean they were going to disappear overnight. But then, she thought, her heart hammering wildly, nor were hers. Was this one of those risks worth taking? Yes, it absolutely was.

'No. Wait,' she said before he could take a further step.

He stilled, his gaze snapping to hers, so wary, so hopeful it made her chest ache.

'I'm sorry too.'

He shook his head and frowned. 'You have nothing to apologise for.'

'I do. I should never have pushed you into talking about something you weren't ready to face.'

'I might never have been ready and I needed to face it.'

'There are things I've also had to face. Things that you've helped me to deal with.'

His jaw clenched, the tiny muscle there on the right pounding away. 'What are you saying?'

She took a deep breath and rose from her chair. 'We could continue to face them together.'

He nodded slowly, once, and her pulse skipped a beat. 'We could.'

'I've missed you.'

'Not nearly as much as I've missed you.'

He opened his arms then and whether she threw herself or he pulled her into them she didn't know. All she knew was that he was kissing her as if his life depended on it, and all her doubts and fears were being swept away on the wave of hot desire and delirious joy that was rushing through her.

'I love you,' he muttered against her mouth as his hold on her loosened. 'Very much.'

'I love you, too.'

'I've been so blind. So stupid. I'm so sorry I hurt you.' He pulled back slightly and the remorse on his face tore at her heart. 'I'll never forgive myself. How can I ever make it up to you?'

'You can start by locking the door.'

'What?'

'Lock the door,' she said again softly as she started to undo the buttons of his shirt just in case there was any lingering confusion. 'And then, my darling, you can show me exactly how sorry you are.'

'Ah, I see,' he said, a glint appearing in his eye as he did as she instructed and then took her in his arms and sat her on her desk. 'I thought you had a meeting.'

Back on the buttons, her whole body vibrating with love and happiness, Orla smiled up at him, leaned forwards and murmured in his ear, 'I lied.'

# EPILOGUE

*The South of France,*
*three months later*

THE LATE SEPTEMBER evening sunshine bathed the privately-owned chateau on the outskirts of Nice in warm golden sunshine. The air was heady with the scent of the lavender that was planted all around, and in the vast, lavishly appointed ballroom five hundred guests had dined on lobster and lamb before parting with millions in the wildly extravagant auction. Ten minutes ago, a band had taken to the stage and the dance floor was filling with men in tuxedos and women in silk.

Out on the terrace that overlooked the city and the sparkling azure Mediterranean beyond, Orla was wrapped in Duarte's arms, eyes closed, smiling softly and swaying to the sultry beat that was drifting out through half a dozen pairs of French doors.

Champagne had been flowing for hours, but she hadn't needed any of it. She was bubbling with happiness and overflowing with love enough as it was.

The last three months had been unbelievably brilliant. Four weeks after Duarte had made all her dreams come true that horrible then fabulous morning in her office, she'd packed up her flat and moved to Porto. She could do her job from anywhere and his apartment needed a cushion or two. When not travelling for work, they spent the weeks in the city and the weekends at the Casa do São Romão.

Today, at lunchtime, they'd flown to Nice for Isabelle Baudelaire's charity ball and checked in to the finest hotel in the city, where they'd idled away most of the afternoon in bed before getting ready.

'One evening of your time,' she murmured against the warm skin of his neck. 'Worth the sacrifice, do you think?'

'Most definitely.'

'Isabelle told me that because of you she sold double the number of tickets she'd expected to and increased the auction donations by half.'

'I'm not sure that was anything to do with me,' he said, the vibrations of his voice sending shivers rippling through her. 'She rivals you for tenacity and skill.'

It was *all* to do with him, she thought dreamily. When he smiled, which he did frequently these days, he was irresistible. 'I wonder who won the trip to the Arctic.'

'I did.'

She leaned back and stared up at him in shock. 'Heavens, why?'

'For the icebergs.'

At the look in his eye, the expression on his face, she went very still and her breath caught. 'What?'

'The Arctic has icebergs,' he said, then frowned. 'But now I think about it, I seem to recall you saying you didn't care much for style-over-substance grand gestures, so that might have been a bad idea. And in any case the trip's in December, and I don't think I can wait that long.'

Her heart thundered and the ground beneath her feet tilted. 'Wait that long to do what?'

'To give you this. I've been carrying it around for days. You should have it before it gets lost.'

'This' was a diamond the shape and size of an almond in a ring of platinum. It sparkled in the setting sun, and when he slid it onto the third finger of her left hand her vision blurred and her throat tightened.

'I love you, Orla,' he said, softly, tenderly. 'More and more each day. Will you marry me?'

She swallowed back the lump in her throat and threw her arms round his neck. 'Yes, of course I will,' she said in between kisses. 'I love you, too. So much.'

'Sorry about the Arctic,' he murmured when they finally broke for air.

'Don't be,' she said, her heart swelling with joy and love. 'It's perfect.'

\* \* \* \* \*

*Head over heels for*
*Undone by Her Ultra-Rich Boss?*
*Then you're sure to get lost in these other*
*Lucy King stories!*

**A Scandal Made in London**
**The Secrets She Must Tell**
**Invitation from the Venetian Billionaire**
**The Billionaire without Rules**

*Available now!*

## #4025 THE BILLIONAIRE'S BABY NEGOTIATION
### by Millie Adams
Innocent Olive Monroe has hated Icelandic billionaire
Gunnar Magnusson for years...and then she discovers the
consequences of their electric night together. Now she's facing
the highest-stakes negotiation of all—Gunnar wants their baby,
her company and Olive!

## #4026 MAID FOR THE GREEK'S RING
### by Louise Fuller
Achileas Kane sees himself as living proof that wedding vows are
meaningless. But this illegitimate son can only gain his inheritance
if he weds. His proposal to hotel chambermaid Effie Price is simply
a contract—until they seal their contract with a single sizzling kiss...

## #4027 THE NIGHT THE KING CLAIMED HER
### by Natalie Anderson
King Felipe knows far too much about the scandalous secrets in
Elsie Wynter's past. But with her stranded in his palace for one
night only, and their mutual desire flaring, he can think of nothing
but finally claiming her...

## #4028 BOUND BY A NINE-MONTH CONFESSION
### by Cathy Williams
Celia is unprepared for the passion she finds with billionaire
Leandro, let alone finding herself holding a positive pregnancy
test weeks later! Now they have nine months to decide if their
connection can make them a family.

HPCNMRA0622

HPCNMRB0622

*Desert prince Akeem wants to show first love Charlotte what she gave up by turning her back on him. Then their secret tryst threatens to become a scandal, and duty-bound Akeem must make an outrageous demand: she'll be his queen!*

*Read on for a sneak preview of*
*Lela May Wight's next story for Harlequin Presents*
His Desert Bride by Demand

"Can you explain what happened?" Akeem asked. "The intensity?"

Could she? Nine years had passed between them—a lifetime—and still… No, she couldn't.

"My father had a lifetime of being reckless for his own amusement—"

"And you wanted a taste of it?"

"No," he denied, his voice a harsh rasp.

"Then what did you want?" Charlotte pushed.

"A night—"

"You risked your reputation for a night?" She cut him off, her insides twisting. "And so far, it's been a disaster, and we haven't even got to bed." She blew out a puff of agitated air.

"Make no mistake," he warned, "things have changed."

"Changed?"

"My bed is off-limits."

She laughed, a throaty gurgle. "How dare you pull me from my life, fly me who knows how many miles into a kingdom I've never heard of and turn my words back on me!" She fixed him with an exasperated glare. "How dare you try to turn the tables on me!"

"If the tables have turned on anyone," he corrected, "it is me because you will be my wife."

*Don't miss*
His Desert Bride by Demand,
*available August 2022 wherever*
*Harlequin Presents books and ebooks are sold.*

Harlequin.com

# Get 4 FREE REWARDS!

**We'll send you 2 FREE Books plus 2 FREE Mystery Gifts.**

**FREE** Value Over **$20**

Both the **Harlequin® Desire** and **Harlequin Presents®** series feature compelling novels filled with passion, sensuality and intriguing scandals.

**YES!** Please send me 2 FREE novels from the Harlequin Desire or Harlequin Presents series and my 2 FREE gifts (gifts are worth about $10 retail). After receiving them, if I don't wish to receive any more books, I can return the shipping statement marked "cancel." If I don't cancel, I will receive 6 brand-new Harlequin Presents Larger-Print books every month and be billed just $5.80 each in the U.S. or $5.99 each in Canada, a savings of at least 11% off the cover price or 6 Harlequin Desire books every month and be billed just $4.55 each in the U.S. or $5.24 each in Canada, a savings of at least 13% off the cover price. It's quite a bargain! Shipping and handling is just 50¢ per book in the U.S. and $1.25 per book in Canada.* I understand that accepting the 2 free books and gifts places me under no obligation to buy anything. I can always return a shipment and cancel at any time. The free books and gifts are mine to keep no matter what I decide.

Choose one: ☐ **Harlequin Desire**
(225/326 HDN GNND)

☐ **Harlequin Presents Larger-Print**
(176/376 HDN GNWY)

Name (please print)

Address                                                                                          Apt. #

City                                          State/Province                          Zip/Postal Code

Email: Please check this box ☐ if you would like to receive newsletters and promotional emails from Harlequin Enterprises ULC and its affiliates. You can unsubscribe anytime.

Mail to the **Harlequin Reader Service:**
**IN U.S.A.:** P.O. Box 1341, Buffalo, NY 14240-8531
**IN CANADA:** P.O. Box 603, Fort Erie, Ontario L2A 5X3

Want to try 2 free books from another series! Call 1-800-873-8635 or visit www.ReaderService.com.